The Neighbor

ALSO BY N.L. HINKENS

THE NEIGHBOR

N.L. HINKENS

JOFFE BOOKS

Joffe Books, London
www.joffebooks.com

First published in Great Britain in 2025

Cover art by Nick Castle

ISBN: 978-1-80573-039-2

For my mother, who faithfully reads all of my books.

CHAPTER 1

I felt it in my gut the first time I met them. Something's off about our new neighbors. My husband, Warren, hates that I watch them through binoculars from behind the heavy linen drapes in our family room. But I feel, in this day and age, it's prudent to know something about the people who live next door to you. Especially when they're inhabiting the fully furnished rental home I invested in after my parents' untimely death in a house fire last year. I'm still gutted about losing them in such a sudden and shocking manner. Mom accidentally left a burner on in the kitchen, and they went to bed oblivious to her fatal, final act. As their only child, I inherited everything, but I would hand it back in a heartbeat to have my parents here with me again.

"Give it a break, Kay. You're making a fool of yourself," Warren grumbles, glancing up from his laptop. "It's illegal in California for landlords to spy on their tenants, not to mention creepy. If they catch you watching them, they might decide to sue us for invasion of privacy."

"I don't believe this!" I gasp, adjusting the focus wheel on the binoculars I told Warren I had purchased for bird watching. "Gary is barbecuing meat on the outdoor grill. It looks

1

like . . . hmm . . . flank steak, or maybe a tri-tip — definitely meat of some kind."

Warren lets out an exasperated snort. "Don't you have anything better to do than give me a running commentary on what the new neighbors are cooking up for dinner?"

I spin around and fire an indignant glare at him. "You're missing the point! Gary turned down the chicken casserole I brought over when they moved in — he said they were vegetarians, remember?"

Warren shrugs disinterestedly. "So what? Would you eat food from someone you don't know the first time you met them? You came on too strong, Kay. You always do. Let them settle in first. They've only been here a few days."

I place the binoculars on the coffee table and flop down on the couch next to Warren with an exaggerated huff. "I don't have a good feeling about them — him, especially. If you lie about the little things, you'll lie about the big things too. I'm pretty sure that's a quote by someone famous, and I couldn't agree more."

"You caught them off guard, that's all. Gary probably couldn't think of a polite way to turn down your casserole on the spur of the moment — he said the first thing that came to mind."

Warren sets aside his laptop and slides over next to me, slinging an arm around my shoulders. "I know you mean well, honey, but Gary told me that he and Beth like to keep to themselves. Not everyone's as sociable as you are. I'm sure they're perfectly nice people. I vetted them, like I told you. Middle-aged, no kids, no pets — what's not to love? Better that they're on the quiet side than too rowdy."

My outrage at the culinary snub is already deflating, but I still feel the need to justify myself. "I was only trying to be neighborly, that's all. I wanted to tell them about the block party next week. I was hoping to get to know them a little beforehand so I could introduce them to a few people — make them feel more welcome. You know me, I just want everyone to get along like one big happy family. And it's my responsibility to keep my finger on the pulse of the neighborhood as president of the Homeowner's Association this year."

Warren squeezes my shoulder. "You're doing a fantastic job of it, with all the ventures you've initiated. Homemade goodies for the seniors, kiddie play dates at the park, winter ping pong league — you've managed to connect people who've lived on the same street for years and barely exchanged two words with one another. I'm sure Gary and Beth will warm up to everyone in no time and fit right in."

I give my husband a tight-lipped smile. The truth is, I'm not so sure I'll be able to warm up to Gary. He made me feel like an idiot standing on his front steps clutching my non-vegetarian casserole — curling his lip at me as if I should have known they didn't eat meat. Apparently, a total fabrication on Gary's part, if what I spotted on his grill is anything to go by.

But that's not the only thing that bothers me about him. There's something sly about the way he looks at me — almost as though he knows my secrets. And I don't like how he keeps finishing his wife's sentences, either, subtly squeezing her arm as he does so. Beth mostly kept her eyes downcast when I went over there to introduce myself. But, as I was leaving, she looked directly at me for a fleeting moment, something unspoken in her eyes. I'm worried she might need help. I have to find a way to strike up a conversation with her when Gary's not around, and try to get her to open up to me. If he's that controlling in public, I dread to think what goes on behind closed doors.

CHAPTER 2

I watch Gary's dark green BMW pull out of his driveway the following morning and wait until his car turns the corner and disappears from view before making my move. I've picked a generous assortment of vegetables from my garden and arranged them in an attractive wicker basket, so my new neighbors won't be able to turn up their noses at my welcome offering this time. I'm sure Beth has already seen the flyer I placed in their mailbox about the upcoming block party, but I want to extend a personal invitation too. It's bound to be intimidating for an introvert like her to meet all the new neighbors at once, and I want to make sure she knows at least one friendly face beforehand.

Warren left for work hours ago, so he can't try to talk me out of my latest attempt to make a connection. Minutes later, I'm standing on our new neighbors' front porch, the laden wicker basket balanced awkwardly on my hip. I might have gone overboard with the zucchini, but it's too late now to make an adjustment. I ring the doorbell and shift my load repeatedly until the door finally cracks open and a wide-eyed Beth peers around it.

"Oh, it's you. I thought it might have been a delivery or something." She gives an embarrassed laugh, gesturing at her

4

flannel robe. "I . . . wasn't expecting visitors. It's not as if we know anyone around here."

I flash her a disarming smile. "I'm sure you've seen the flyer about the block party already. It will be the perfect opportunity to meet people."

Beth attempts a smile in return, but looks half frozen with fear at the prospect.

"We have a bunch of great folks on this street," I assure her. "Trust me, it won't take long to get to know everyone." I gesture to the overflowing basket digging into my side. "I brought you some fresh vegetables from my garden."

"Thank you. I . . . um . . ." She picks at the collar of her robe, an uncertain look flitting across her face as she glances fearfully over my shoulder. "Would you . . . like to come in?"

She makes no attempt to pull the door open any farther, as though signaling she'd rather I turned down her distinctly unenthusiastic invitation. But I haven't accomplished what I came here to do yet. I'm determined to befriend her and let her know I'm happy to lend an ear — or my help, if she needs it. Moving to a new area can be lonely at the best of times, and I hate the thought of her being trapped in a controlling relationship with no one to talk to about it. Maybe I'm jumping to conclusions, but I'd sooner trust my instincts than ignore them. "Thanks, Beth, I would love to come in for a few minutes."

I heave a sigh of relief when the door finally swings open. If I don't set this basket down soon, my arms are going to cease to function.

"You'll have to excuse my appearance," Beth mumbles apologetically, as she shuffles to the kitchen in her fluffy sheepskin slippers. "I haven't had a chance to get dressed this morning."

I glance into the family room in passing. It doesn't look as though they've made any attempt to personalize the space. All the shelves are bare. No photos, books, decor, or accessories of any kind in sight. Maybe they haven't got around to unpacking all their boxes yet. I can't imagine what Beth has been doing for the past few days, but she seems the type to be easily overwhelmed.

I set the basket of vegetables down on the kitchen island, my gaze drifting to an empty bottle of vodka next to a half-full shot glass on the counter. I fight to keep my expression neutral even as my brain goes into overdrive. Surely she hasn't been drinking already this morning. Is that why she's still wandering around the house in her robe with a dazed look on her face?

"You must have a green thumb," Beth says, fiddling with a strand of her shoddily bleached hair. "These vegetables look delicious."

"I have to admit, it's become a bit of a hobby of mine. There's plenty more where those came from. I'm sure you must go through a lot of vegetables in your recipes. You'll have to share some of your favorites with me."

Beth throws me a strange look. "I'm not much of a cook, to be honest."

"Really? Something smelled awfully good on the grill last night. Was that Gary?"

"Um, yes." Beth blinks and looks away. "Would you like something to drink?"

"I'd love a cup of coffee, if you have decaf. I can only do one mug of caffeine in the mornings. Warren says it hypes me up too much." I give her a conspiratorial wink. "Husbands, eh? Think they know it all."

She doesn't take the bait, but I see a flash of trepidation in her eyes before she turns her back on me.

I slide onto a barstool at the island while Beth busies herself with the coffee maker.

"So, tell me about this block party," she says, setting a steaming mug in front of me. She pulls out the stool next to me and sits down. Up close, her face is lined and haggard, as though she's had a hard life. Or maybe it's because she's a closet drinker. I'm not thrilled at the thought of renting my house out to an alcoholic and dealing with all the problems that could potentially stem from that. Warren may have vetted our new renters, but it's not as though he could ask them about their average weekly consumption of alcohol.

"It's a potluck," I reply. "Everyone brings their favorite family recipes — feel free to bring a vegetarian one. We have games for the kids — sidewalk chalk, bubbles, face painting, and a scavenger hunt for the teenagers. Corn toss and ping pong. There's always a bake-off competition, and the winner takes home the block trophy each year. We all wear name tags and write our professions and hobbies on them — it's a good way to break the ice for the new folks like yourselves."

Beth wraps her fingers tighter around her mug. I can't help but notice the tremor in her hand. I was hoping to put her at ease, but it appears my description of our activity-filled block party has had the opposite effect. Maybe she has social anxiety. That could have been why Gary was finishing her sentences for her. I should probably give him the benefit of the doubt, until I know more about them.

"It must be a lot of work to organize," Beth says, wrinkling her brow.

"It's not too bad, actually. We have to get a permit from the city to close the street, of course, but we've been doing it for several years now, so we have a spreadsheet of what needs to be done. Everyone pitches in, and my friend Amber, who lives a few doors down from me, is a huge help."

Amber is also my confidante, and I've already had a conversation with her about my less-than-favorable first impression of my renters. She thinks I'm rushing to judgement.

"Have you met any of the other neighbors?" I ask.

Beth takes a hasty gulp of her coffee. "No. I've . . . been so busy. I haven't had a chance to venture out of the house."

As shocking as her admission is, I half suspected as much. I've never seen her in the backyard or going in and out of her front door. Admittedly, I'm not here 24/7 to monitor her comings and goings, but I rate myself as a reasonably proficient private eye when I am home. "I'd be happy to invite a couple of the other women over for lunch so you can meet them."

Beth splutters a mouthful of coffee. "No! I mean . . . no rush, thanks. I'll wait for the block party. I still have a lot of things to sort out, as you can imagine."

I beam at her to try to ease her obvious distress. "If I can give you a hand with anything, let me know. And be sure to tell Gary that Warren has plenty of tools if you guys need to borrow anything."

Beth peers at me curiously over the rim of her coffee mug. "How long have you and Warren been married?"

"Twenty-two years this September. How about you?"

"Almost three years." She frowns, dropping her gaze. "Gary was . . . married before."

I'm not sure why she randomly brought that up. Maybe she felt she had to explain why they got married later in life. I'm guessing they're in their early fifties, a decade or so older than Warren and myself. I can't imagine what Beth ever saw in Gary that convinced her to marry him. At the very least, he's controlling. I'm trying not to entertain the worst-case scenario — maybe Gary is only looking out for his insecure wife. I wonder if Beth was married before too. She seems like the type to jump from one emotionally abusive relationship to another — unassertive and beaten down. She could be hiding bruises beneath her robe, for all I know. But that's speculation. I need to get her to trust me before she'll open up about any secrets she might be hiding.

"How did you and Gary meet?" I ask with a light-hearted smile.

She grimaces. "At a grief group." She raises her mug to her lips and slurps a small sip.

I'm shocked into silence. I was expecting her to tell me that they'd met online, like so many people do nowadays, or maybe through mutual friends. I let a moment unwind long enough for her to volunteer more details. Did Gary's first wife die, or is he divorced? I don't know Beth well enough to press her on the topic. I'd like to ask if either of them has kids, but it's a risky question, considering how they met. I know more than I care to about loss.

She sets down her mug with a *thunk* and pins a searching gaze on me. "Do you have children?"

My skin prickles. It's almost as though she's been reading my thoughts. "Unfortunately, no. I had a couple of miscarriages. Warren and I weren't able to have kids."

Beth turns and stares out the kitchen window, a faraway look in her eyes. "I lost my only child. A daughter. She was just nineteen."

I squirm in my seat, blindsided at the abrupt and disturbing revelation. "I'm . . . so sorry, Beth. I can't imagine how painful that must have been."

She bites her bottom lip. "You mustn't tell anyone I told you."

I blink, disturbed by the sheer panic contorting her face.

I reach over and lay a hand on her trembling arm. "Beth, you can trust me. I won't mention it to any of the other neighbors, if you don't want me to."

"It's not the neighbors I'm worried about. It's him." She leans toward me, a manic look in her eyes. "He thinks I'm crazy."

CHAPTER 3

"Of course you're not crazy," I say, trying to tamp down my outrage at Gary's insensitivity. "Losing a child is about the most traumatic thing that can happen to a person. It's natural to struggle to come to terms with it."

"You don't understand." Beth buries her face in her hands, her shoulders shuddering. "Gary says she's not dead."

I frown, not entirely sure I heard her right. It sounds like an extraordinarily cruel thing for her husband to say. But I shouldn't question his motives without some context. My first impression of Beth is that she's emotionally fragile. Maybe Gary feels she can't handle the truth. Or maybe she's confused — she seems a bit out of it. "Why would he say that?" I ask in a cautious tone.

"Forget it. I shouldn't have said anything." She gets to her feet abruptly and rinses out her mug at the sink, indicating that our coffee klatsch session is over.

I carry my mug over to her, and she snatches it out of my hands as though eager to expedite my departure.

"Beth, if you ever need to talk, I'm here for you," I say gently.

She makes no attempt to revive the conversation, so I thank her for the coffee and take my leave.

Back in my own house, I sink down on the couch and sift through our conversation in my mind. I don't know what to make of it. Why would Gary tell Beth that her daughter isn't dead? Does he really believe that? Surely it's not a matter of debate — there must be a death certificate somewhere. Could Gary be gaslighting her for some sick purpose only he understands? Or is Beth really crazy? She sounded rational enough when we were talking, but the empty vodka bottle I spotted gives me pause. Is she a closet alcoholic? Did she turn to drink for solace after her daughter died?

And why was Gary at the grief group? Did he have a legitimate reason to be there, or was he preying on vulnerable women? Beth mentioned that he'd been married before. Maybe his first wife died. A shiver crosses my shoulders when I think about our initial meeting and the sly look he gave me. As crazy as it sounds, I can't quash the needling thought that Gary might have had something to do with his first wife's death.

I fish my phone from my pocket and text Amber to ask if she can meet for lunch. I need to bounce all this off her and see what she makes of it. I promised Beth I wouldn't mention the loss of her daughter to the neighbors, but I don't consider it gossiping when my only motive is to help her. Besides, I can trust Amber to keep a secret.

After arranging to meet Amber at a local Mexican restaurant, I put on a load of laundry, then settle down at my computer and get to work. I love my part-time job as a health care project manager, overseeing budgets and timelines, and making sure my team members are happy and staying on task. Coordinating projects and leading people comes naturally to me, which is why I enjoy organizing the neighborhood block party and managing the HOA. I'm glad Warren recognizes how capable I am and is proud of me. I can't imagine being married to someone like Gary — condescending and controlling, happy to settle for a browbeaten wife who's a nervous wreck in his presence.

I'm about to break for lunch when my phone chirps with an incoming text. I glance at it, my interest piqued when I

11

see it's from Gary. I tap the message and read it in growing bewilderment.

Beth was extremely distraught when I called her a few minutes ago. She has a hard time coping with strangers and doesn't do well with change. I would appreciate it if you don't go next door when I'm not home.

I stare at the text in disbelief for several minutes, alternating between shock and rage, while trying to decide how to respond. Maybe Gary can bully his wife into submission, but he has another thing coming if he thinks he can shut me down. I have every right to visit whomever I want to. This only confirms my suspicions about his controlling nature. If he doesn't want Beth speaking freely to me, there has to be a good reason why. It just makes me more determined to get to the bottom of it.

I'm late arriving at Marco's Taqueria. Amber arches a questioning brow when she spots me hurrying over to the vinyl booth she's seated in. "Busy morning?" she says, quirking a grin.

"Sorry, I was just getting ready to leave the house when I got a strange text."

The waiter bounces over to us, pen and pad at the ready, and we order our favorite trio of tacos.

"So, what's this strange text about?" Amber asks, dipping a chip into the bowl of salsa in front of her.

I reach for my glass and gulp down a mouthful of water. "I'll get to that. Remember I told you I wasn't sure if I liked our new renters?"

She lets out a chortle. "That's putting it mildly. As I recall, you thought Gary was a jerk and Beth was a pushover."

My cheeks heat up. "To be fair, you asked me to summarize them in one word. Anyway, there's more to it than that. I think he's being emotionally abusive. He manipulates her."

Amber squeezes her lemon wedge into her water. "Are you sure you're not jumping to conclusions? I know what a savior complex you have. You always want to dive in and rescue everyone."

I twist my lips into a mock scowl. "At least I'm vigilant. I hate to see people being mistreated. Anyway, hear me out.

12

I brought Beth some vegetables from my garden earlier. She wasn't going to let me in at first — barely cracked the door open three inches. And check this out. She says she hasn't left the house since she moved in a week ago. Don't you think that's weird?"

Amber shrugs. "Unusual, sure, but she's probably been busy unpacking. Has her car not moved at all?"

"Not that I know of. Come to think of it, I'm not sure she has a car. I haven't seen one, other than the BMW Gary drives to work. I'm beginning to think she's not allowed to leave the house while he's at work."

Amber shakes her head. "You're reading too much into it. Lots of people share a car. If she works from home, she might not need one."

"I don't know that she works at all. I don't want to judge her, but I spotted an empty vodka bottle and a half-full shot glass on her kitchen counter this morning."

Amber throws me a startled look, just as the waiter reappears and sets our food in front of us.

I unwrap my silverware and place my napkin on my lap. "I'm thinking she might have lost her driver's license. DUI or something."

"I suppose it's possible," Amber says, reaching for a beef taco and tucking in.

"There's more," I say, swallowing a mouthful of shrimp. "But keep this to yourself. Beth asked me if I had any children, and then she shared that she'd lost her nineteen-year-old daughter. But get this, she warned me not to let Gary know that she'd told me."

Amber wrinkles her brow. "Why ever not? Was he responsible for her death or something?"

I wipe my lips on a napkin. "Beth told me that Gary thinks she's crazy. He says her daughter's not dead."

Amber's mouth drops open. "That's messed up. Is he gaslighting her or is she actually cuckoo?"

"I don't know. That's what I need you to help me figure out. I don't know who to believe." I pull up the message from

Gary on my phone and show it to her. "This is what Gary sent me just as I was about to head out the door. What do you make of it?"

Amber reads it through and lets out a low whistle. "That's pretty direct. But maybe he's just looking out for his wife's welfare if she's . . . you know." She twirls her finger around her right temple.

I give a sharp shake of my head. "I'm not buying it. If he really cared about Beth's well-being, he would have asked me to check up on her while he was at work. Something doesn't sit right with me. I'm afraid Beth might be in danger."

CHAPTER 4

The block party is in full swing and, judging by the laughter ringing out all around me, the steady buzz of conversation, and the easy smiles on everyone's faces, it's turning out to be every bit the success I orchestrated it to be. Even the weather is cooperating — a balmy seventy-five degrees. Not bad for April in southern California.

Despite the level of satisfaction I feel at a job well done, I can't ignore the twinge of disappointment that, in spite of my valiant efforts, Gary and Beth haven't bothered to show up. Their green BMW is parked in the driveway, so obviously they're home. I felt sure they would have wanted to avail of the opportunity to meet their new neighbors in a casual and welcoming setting. Instead, they've opted out, opening themselves up to adverse speculation. I'm having to field a battery of questions I'm ill-equipped to answer as I serve up paper plates of BBQ chicken and tri-tip at my station next to Amber's.

"What's up with your renters?"

"Don't they want to mingle with us lesser mortals?"

"Did they get an invite?"

"Are they out of town?"

"Don't tell me they're germaphobes or something?"

15

I do my best to fob my neighbors off by mumbling excuses about Gary and Beth likely being exhausted after their big move, and not up for a raucous party and a barrage of introductions.

"Do you want me to go knock on their door?" Amber offers, as she refills the drink dispensers with iced tea and lemonade.

"No. I've invited them multiple times already. I don't want them to think I'm harassing them. Besides, they can't help but see what's going on out here. Obviously, they don't want to participate." I shoot Amber a loaded look. "I just hope Gary's not preventing Beth from coming to punish her for inviting me over."

"How did he know you were there in the first place?" Amber asks, as she helps a young child fill his paper cup with lemonade.

I let out a snort. "Good question. He pestered Warren to install an outdoor security camera before he agreed to rent the place — now I know why. He has the app on his phone. He probably got a notification that I'd shown up at the front door. Evidently, he doesn't want Beth having visitors he doesn't know about."

"Speaking of someone showing up," Amber mutters, elbowing me in the ribs.

I look up from the chafing dish I'm refilling with chili beans to see Gary and Beth strolling down the street toward the festivities. A couple of the neighbors intercept them, and they shake hands. I can't hear what they're saying, but they're smiling and laughing, which is a good sign that they're making an effort to socialize. Maybe they were just finishing up a project at the house, or perhaps Beth needed to build up the courage to join us.

I can't leave my busy station to greet them, but every so often I throw a surreptitious glance in their direction as they meander through the crowd. Beth clutches a plastic cup of wine in one hand, and Gary remains glued to her side, almost as though he's guiding her. I'm not sure if she arrived at the party drunk and he's afraid she might take a tumble, or if he's just hovering to make sure she doesn't say anything she's not supposed to.

Eventually, they make their way to the serving tables and join the line for food.

I beam at them when they reach my station. "Hi there! I'm so glad you could make it! What can I get you? Salad, coleslaw, and beans sound good?"

Gary points to the meat. "I'll have some of your delicious-looking tri-tip and BBQ chicken. Beth's the diehard vegetarian."

Her head instantly swivels in his direction. "No, I'm—" She's about to say something more, but then changes her mind and takes a hasty gulp of wine instead.

I throw her a sympathetic look, trying to convey my support, as I pile her plate with an ample portion of vegetarian items. It's all I can do to bite my tongue. Is this Gary's way of controlling her, by telling her what she can and cannot eat? I hope she knows that all she has to do is ask and I'll help her in whatever way I can. Until then, there's not much I can do without coming across as interfering. "This is my good friend Amber," I say, gesturing to her as Gary and Beth move on to the drinks station.

Amber pulls a sweaty strand of auburn hair from her forehead and tucks it behind her ear. "Nice to meet you both. Kay's told me all about you. How are you settling in?"

Beth shoots me a wary glance, as though second-guessing whether she can trust me to keep my mouth shut. "It's a bit—"

"Great, thanks," Gary cuts in, gripping his wife's arm a little more tightly.

"What brought you to Santa Morelos?" Amber asks, her bright smile belying the motivation behind the question.

"We needed a change," Gary says, in a vague tone clearly designed to shut down Amber's line of inquiry.

I break the awkward silence that ensues. "Beth, how about Amber and I take you to lunch at our favorite Mexican

17

restaurant on Monday? Let's shoot for noon, if that works for you." I can't imagine why it wouldn't. It's not as if she ever goes anywhere.

She stares down at her wine glass as though searching in the dregs for a response. "Um, I have a doctor's appointment."

"Not a problem," I counter. "You can drive yourself and we can meet you in town afterward. We're flexible on time."

Gary clears his throat. "Beth doesn't drive. She hit a deer a year or so ago and it knocked her confidence. I'll be taking her to her appointment."

Before I have a chance to respond, he whisks her off to the picnic tables so abruptly that she almost trips on the curb.

"Charming! Told you he was controlling," I mutter through clenched teeth. "Now you've seen it with your own eyes."

Amber turns to me, visibly affronted. "That goes without saying. He made it clear he doesn't want Beth hanging out with us." She glances over at them as they settle into their seats. "Did you believe that story about the deer?"

I ladle out a plateful of food for the next person in line and wait until they move out of earshot before responding. "It's possible. They might even have moved because of Beth's drinking — fresh start and all. I think losing her daughter really did a number on her."

I slap a spoonful of beans onto a plate a little too forcefully and some of the sauce splatters all over the place. "Whoops! Sorry about that," I say to the teenager in front of me, who's too busy staring at his phone to notice what I've done.

"It's weird that Gary drives her everywhere, but maybe he's just being overprotective — trying to cover for her drinking," Amber says.

I lower my voice. "Or he could be the cause of it. I think Beth's scared of him. What if he was responsible for her daughter's death?"

CHAPTER 5

I'm just about to put my feet up after spending the last couple of hours cleaning up the remnants of another successful block party when my phone rings.

"Ugh, don't answer it," Warren pleads. He's stretched out on the couch with a cushion over his face, exhausted after supervising twenty-five teenagers on a scavenger hunt. "We'll handle the distress calls about lost property and suggestions for next year's party tomorrow. They can leave a voicemail."

I grimace. "I have to take this. It's Mrs. Torres. She might need my help with something." My elderly neighbor, Maria Torres, lives alone with her two cats in the house on the other side of Gary and Beth's place. She's fiercely independent and still drives her silver Oldsmobile — a terrifying concept, considering how bad her eyesight is. We all keep watch over her in our own discreet ways, but I've never felt more responsible for her than I do this year as the HOA president. It would be delinquent of me not to take her call.

"Hi, Maria. Did you have a good time at the block party?"

"It was wonderful as always, Kay. You must be tired after all the work you put into it. How did our new neighbors enjoy it?"

19

"I think they had a good time," I reply, trying to erase the image from my mind of Gary jerking Beth's arm so hard she almost tripped.

Maria lets out a disapproving *humph*. "I don't like the way that man treats his wife. I told him he needed to mind his manners. He kept interrupting when I was trying to talk to her, cutting her off and answering questions on her behalf."

"He does seem a bit controlling," I agree. "Amber and I tried to set up a lunch date with Beth, and he shut us down."

"Well, I'm ninety-two years old; he can't shut me down. I'll pop by when he's at work and invite her over for lunch." Maria clears her throat before continuing. "But that's not the reason I'm calling. I hate to bother you with this, but the policeman who came by earlier told me I should alert the homeowner's association."

I kick my footstool aside and straighten up on my chair. "Police? Are you okay, Maria?"

"Yes, I'm fine, but my house was broken into during the block party." She gives an apologetic laugh. "Well, the truth is, I left the back door unlocked. Someone came in and stole my purse. But what really upset me is that they left the door open, and Smokey and Flora have disappeared. I was hoping you could send out one of those group emails you do and ask if anyone's seen them."

"Yes, of course. I'll do it right away. I'm so sorry, Maria."

"I blame myself for leaving the door unlocked. But who would have thought such a thing would happen? There were no strangers around with the street being closed. Whoever did it must have come in on foot and snuck out through the back garden and over the fence."

No strangers around. My skin prickles as I weigh her words. That's not entirely accurate. Gary and Beth are as good as strangers. And they showed up to the block party late. Could they have gone into Maria's house and stolen her purse? I shake my head free of the improbable thought. Why would they do something like that? I'm not even certain there was a break-in. It's possible Maria left the back door open herself and simply misplaced her purse.

"Are you sure your purse is gone? Did you look in your car?"

"Yes. I've looked everywhere. The police helped me search the house too. I'm sure I left my purse in the same place I always leave it."

"What does it look like? I'll include a description in the email."

"It's an ivory shoulder bag with a gold zipper."

"Got it. Do you need me to help you cancel your credit cards?"

"Thank you, dear, but I already took care of that. That's the first thing the police told me to do."

"That's good. Did you have any cash in your purse?"

Maria lets out a doleful sigh. "Eighty dollars. I know that's not a lot of money to some people, but I was planning on going to the grocery store tomorrow."

"Do you need some cash to tide you over?"

"That's very kind, but I have my emergency fund hidden in the—"

"That's okay! I don't want to know where you keep your money, Maria. You really shouldn't be telling people stuff like that. I'll send that email out right away. Call me if you need anything."

Warren is propped up on one elbow, eying me curiously. "What's going on?"

I recount what happened as I wait for my laptop to power up.

"Wow! Hard to believe that happened right under our noses," he says, squeezing his chin thoughtfully. "I wonder if any other houses were hit at the same time."

"Guess we'll find out once this makes the rounds. Hopefully, her cats show up soon. That's what she's most worried about." I turn my attention to composing a quick email and sending it out to everyone on the block party invite list. Within minutes, the responses start flooding in.

Is Maria okay? She wasn't hurt, was she?

I'm going out right now to look for her cats.

I'll swing by her place and make sure she has everything she needs.

I can't believe that happened on our street. I'm checking my jewelry to make sure nothing was stolen from our house.

Tell Maria she's welcome to stay at our place tonight if she feels unsafe.

I'm heartened by the responses. As usual, everyone is rallying together — well, almost everyone. I can't help but notice that Gary and Beth haven't responded, but I assume not everyone has had a chance to read the email yet. I need to give them the benefit of the doubt. But I have my antenna up.

They're still strangers, after all.

CHAPTER 6

I've been keeping a close eye on things next door and haven't seen Beth come out of her house in the three days since the block party. I'm growing increasingly worried, so I decide to pay her another visit when I take a break for lunch. I've been mulling over the discrepancy between what Beth believes about her daughter and what Gary told her, and I won't be able to rest until I get to the truth. I'm not convinced that Gary has his wife's best interests at heart. Something about their relationship isn't adding up. As incredible as it seems to think that Gary might have preyed on Beth in the grief group and is now gaslighting her by pretending her daughter isn't dead, I wouldn't put it past him. The question is, why? Does he get a kick out of the power he wields by throwing her mentally and emotionally off balance, or is there some other reason? Whatever the case, Beth needs my help. She's not capable of standing up to someone as domineering as Gary.

I pocket my phone before going next door. I don't care if Gary gets an alert that I'm standing on his front doorstep again, defying his express wishes not to go over there when he's not home. What can he do about it — call the police? I'm hardly a threat, just a friendly neighbor and landlord checking up on my tenant. I care about Beth, just like I care about all my neighbors.

I've been checking up on Maria Torres too, ever since the break-in, just so she knows she's not alone. Thankfully, both her cats were located and returned to her within a couple of hours. Still no sign of her purse, though. It's not the kind of thing that typically happens in our neighborhood, so we're all a little bit more wary of strangers and unfamiliar cars these days.

I ring Beth's doorbell multiple times but get no response, so I walk around to the back of the house and tent my fingers over my eyes to peer through the kitchen window. I let out a gasp at the sight that greets me. Beth is slumped over at the table, head resting on her hands. For a terrifying moment, I think she might be dead, but she startles upright when I bang on the window to get her attention. She struggles to get to her feet, swaying unsteadily as she shuffles over to the back door. I hold my breath the entire time, praying she doesn't fall.

The door inches open. "You can't come in," she mumbles.

I try to mask my shock at her thready voice. It sounds as though she's slurring her words. "Beth, are you okay? You don't look well. Let me make you some coffee." I attempt to squeeze past her, but she's surprisingly quick and blocks the door with her foot. "No! I'll call the police," she hisses.

I raise my palms and back away. "I only want to help—"

The words die on my lips when she slams the door in my face with a resounding crack. I wouldn't be surprised if she's damaged it. After standing there for a moment in stunned silence, I stomp back to my house trying to make sense of Beth's hostile reaction. Did Gary threaten her if she disobeys his order not to let me in? It's heartbreaking to think that he forces her to spend all day on her own, closed up in the house. Does he not realize she's developed a drinking problem — trying to soothe her grief, no doubt?

After mulling it over for most of the afternoon, I decide I'd be shirking my responsibility if I didn't confront Gary about my concerns for Beth's welfare. I make sure to be lurking in my front yard when he arrives home from work later that day.

"Hey, Gary," I say, popping my head up from the planter I'm weeding. "I haven't had a chance to talk to you since the block party. Hopefully, you and Beth are all settled in now. Is everything okay with the rental house? Is there anything you need Warren to take a look at?"

Gary gives a brusque nod of acknowledgment as he presses the key fob to lock his car. "Everything's fine, thank you."

He starts to walk away, and I call after him. "I haven't seen Beth in a few days. She's not sick, is she? I know she had a doctor's appointment recently."

He wheels around to face me, his countenance darkening.

I can feel my hackles rising as he continues to glare at me. Beneath his veneer of control, he's an angry man, but he doesn't intimidate me, if that's what he's trying to do. And if he's abusing his wife, it's time I had it out with him. I let my trowel drop in the dirt and yank off my gloves. "I might as well tell you — you'll see it on your camera anyway, if you haven't already — I went over to your place today to check on Beth, and she didn't look well at all. She seemed very stressed out, and she was unsteady on her feet, like she was drunk or something. I don't mean to intrude, Gary, but I'm worried about her spending so much time alone while you're at work. I think she needs help, but she wouldn't let me in — I suspect she was terrified you would find out. You can't keep isolating her like you do."

A slow flush creeps up his neck. For a long moment, he says nothing. I brace myself for the unexpected, half afraid he's gearing up to lash out at me, verbally or physically, or maybe both, but then he exhales a long breath and wipes a hand across his brow. "I know how it looks, but it's not what you think. Beth suffers from clinical depression. She's on some heavy-duty medication. Her appointment the other day was with a psychiatrist."

I bite my lip, absorbing what he's telling me and trying to decide if I believe him. Beth did seem very low when she told me about losing her daughter. If she's taking medication, and mixing it with alcohol, it would explain why she seems so out of it. It makes me even more upset with Gary for knowingly leaving her alone for long periods of time like he does. But I don't want to come across as a judgmental neighbor, now that he's opening up to me. Empathy is called for first. "I'm sorry to hear that. Her daughter's death must have been very traumatic for her."

Gary places his briefcase on the fence post and leans his elbows on it, holding my gaze. "Just to be clear, her daughter, Luna, isn't dead. She left because she was fed up with her mother refusing to get help for her addiction to alcohol and prescription drugs. Luna broke off all contact. We have no idea where she's living these days."

My jaw drops at this bombshell. How could Beth have lied to me like that? Was she too embarrassed to tell me the truth? Or is she so far gone that she actually believes her daughter is dead?

"I'm at my wits' end," Gary goes on, running his fingers through his hair. "I've confiscated her car keys and taken control of our finances. She was running up debts to buy pills on the street. She's even been caught shoplifting, and I can't tell you how many times she's made a scene in public. The last time it happened, she earned herself a misdemeanor for disorderly conduct." He gives a sheepish shrug. "If you must know, it's the reason we moved — to make a fresh start. I've done my best to shield her from the consequences of her actions, but it's hard to make friends, and easy to lose them. People don't understand; they get their feelings hurt. It's easier just to keep to ourselves."

My mind is reeling at the admission. Apparently, we've unwittingly rented our house out to an alcoholic and a druggie. I suddenly think of Maria's missing purse. Could Beth have taken it — looking for cash to support her habit? Given

26

what Gary is telling me, it seems the most likely explanation. "Did you see the email I sent out about Maria Torres's purse being stolen?" I ask.

Gary gives a tired nod. "I know what you're thinking. I already asked Beth about it. She swears she didn't take it."

I don't comment on Beth's denial. It proves nothing, as far as I'm concerned. Everyone knows addicts are prolific liars.

"So, are you going to evict us now that you know the full story?" Gary asks, yanking me out of my reverie.

"What? No! Of course not! I'm glad you confided in me. It certainly clears things up. If Beth is sick and needs help, the last thing I want to do is destabilize her living situation." I hope my tone sounds more convincing than I feel on the inside. The minute Warren gets wind of this, he'll want to evict them as quickly as possible. I can already hear his voice in my head.

We're not living next door to a junkie with a misdemeanor. Crime begets crime. Where do you think it will end? If they have financial problems, we'll never be able to get rid of them if they stop paying the rent.

"Best not to mention any of this to my husband," I say. "He may not be comfortable with the situation. I won't discuss it with anyone else either. It sounds as though Beth is already getting professional help, so I have no objections to you continuing to rent the house. But if I find out there are drugs on the premises, or exchanging hands on our street, it will change everything."

Gary gives a relieved nod. "Absolutely. Thank you, and I appreciate your discretion." He picks up his briefcase and turns to go into the house.

"Wait!" I call after him. "That email you sent me about staying away from Beth. I'd still like to reach out to her. Sounds like she could use a friend. How about I take her to lunch tomorrow?"

Gary traces his fingers across his brow. "I don't think that's a good idea. She doesn't handle unfamiliar surroundings well."

"I promise I'll bring her straight home afterward — sooner, if she's uncomfortable."

He frowns, thinking it over for a moment or two. "All right, but under one condition. Don't mention her daughter. The topic always sends her into a downward spiral. Trust me, you don't want to witness it. She's very fragile emotionally. And if anything happens to her, it's on your head."

CHAPTER 7

I pull up next door around noon to pick up Beth. Gary told me she doesn't like Mexican, so I've arranged to take her to my favorite trattoria in town for lunch instead and invited Amber to join us. Amber's pretty astute when it comes to people, and I want her to get a good read on Beth and see what she makes of her. Gary's explanation of his wife's behavior made sense in the moment, but after sleeping on it, I'm not sure he was totally up front with me. In fact, I'm questioning everything he told me. There are too many things that don't add up. If he knows his wife has a problem with alcohol, why is he buying it for her? It's not as if Beth can drive herself to the store. By his own admission, he confiscated her car keys and took control of her finances. Today, I want to give Beth a chance to explain her side of things. But I'll have to tread carefully. She does appear to be fragile, so I can't risk pushing her over the edge.

After ringing her doorbell for the third time, I knock sharply on the glass inset on the front door. I can't imagine what's taking her so long to answer. I texted her earlier to confirm our lunch date and she responded with a thumbs-up emoji. Hopefully, she hasn't drunk herself into a stupor and fallen asleep somewhere. When she finally comes to the door, she peers quizzically at me. To my dismay, she's dressed in stained sweats and a baggy T-shirt. The blank look on her face says it all.

"Did you forget that we're going to lunch with Amber?" I ask, trying not to sound as frustrated as I feel.

She claps a hand to her mouth. "I don't believe it! I totally lost track of what day it is." She gives a despairing shake of her head. "I really don't know what I'm doing anymore. Give me a couple of minutes and I'll change." She throws me a pleading look and I smile back reassuringly.

"Take your time. I'll just text Amber to let her know we're running late."

Ten minutes later, we're buckled into my Lexus and ready to go. Beth looks marginally better with her hair combed and tied back from her face, but I notice her hand shakes as she latches her seatbelt. I wonder if she's been drinking this morning.

"I really am sorry," she says, as I pull out onto the street. "I completely spaced on our lunch date."

I give her a bemused look. "But you responded to my text earlier — you even gave it a thumbs-up."

She frowns as she fishes a pair of sunglasses from her bulging purse. I can't help wondering what she's lugging with her, when all we're doing is going out to lunch and straight home afterward.

"I must have misplaced my phone after I texted you," Beth responds. "I keep doing the stupidest things lately. I accidentally deleted a bunch of contacts in my phone the other day, old friends I've known for years — even the number for my sister in Oregon. Gary gets so frustrated with me. He complains when I leave things in strange places. I told him it's because it's a new house and I still don't know my way around, but that's hardly an excuse for putting my iPad in the fridge."

I throw her a look of alarm. "That does sound concerning. You might want to talk to your doctor about your medication."

She blinks at me, a blank look on her face. "What medication?"

I swallow, gripping the steering wheel a little tighter. I don't know how she'll react when she finds out I've been talking about her mental health behind her back. "Gary mentioned you were taking something for depression."

She elevates her brows. "Really?"

I scrunch my face in concentration as I navigate through a busy intersection. Surely, she must know if she's taking medication. Is she just pretending to be confused? Or is she too embarrassed to admit to needing help? "It's nothing to be ashamed of," I say. "I was on antidepressants for a while after my last miscarriage."

Beth turns and looks out the window. "I don't know what Gary's talking about. I haven't been prescribed anything."

I press my lips together in irritation. I can't keep ignoring the obvious. "Beth, are you drinking? I saw an empty vodka bottle in your kitchen the first time I came over."

She sighs. "I don't drink anymore."

I bite my lip, struggling to come up with a response that won't sound like I'm accusing her of lying. Is she living in an alternate universe, in denial about everything, including her own daughter shutting her out of her life? I'm tempted to tell her I know about the prescription pills, and that she's been caught shoplifting, but it won't encourage her to trust me. And I need her to trust me so I can get to the bottom of what's going on next door.

"Gary's worried about you," I say, as I pull into the restaurant parking lot and switch off the engine.

She laughs, but the expression on her face is pained. "He's worried I'll leave him, you mean. He's done everything in his power to make sure I can't."

My heart begins to thud a little harder. "Like what?"

She tugs at her sleeve, avoiding my gaze.

I lay a comforting hand on her arm. "You know you don't have to stay with him, Beth. You're not his prisoner."

Her head droops. "I couldn't leave him now even if I wanted to. I have no job, no money, no car — thanks to him."

"He was only looking out for you when he took your car keys. You said yourself you've been doing strange things lately. You don't want to black out when you're behind the wheel. Is that what happened when you hit the deer?"

She throws me an odd look. "I didn't hit a deer. Gary was driving when that happened."

I hold her gaze for a moment longer, before deciding not to argue the point. It isn't something I can get to the bottom of with any degree of certainty. It's a he-said-she-said scenario. I need to focus on getting to know Beth a little better before I can decide if she's living in a make-believe world, or if Gary is gaslighting her.

All I know for sure is that one of my renters is lying to me. And I intend to find out why.

CHAPTER 8

"Sorry to keep you waiting," I say, pulling out a chair at the table where Amber is already sipping on an iced tea.

"Not a problem." She smiles at Beth. "It's good to see you again. How did you enjoy the block party?"

"It was a bit overwhelming," Beth replies, fidgeting with the strap of her purse. "But everyone was very welcoming." She takes her seat and fixates on the menu as though she hasn't seen food in months. "What do you recommend?"

"They make a mean Tuscan chicken and bacon panini here," I say. "Or if you're looking for something vegetarian, the strawberry goat cheese salad is excellent."

"I think I'll go for the panini," Beth says. "I'm starving. I didn't have anything to eat this morning other than the smoothie Gary made me at six."

So much for being vegetarian. Sounds like it was just Gary trying to control her again.

Amber arches a brow. "I wish I had a husband like that. Mine doesn't even know how to boil an egg."

"Gary makes me a mango, spinach, and flaxseed smoothie every morning," Beth says, her eyes still skimming the menu longingly. "He always makes sure I drink it before he leaves for work — he worries about my health." She lets out a strained laugh. "To be honest, I'd much rather have waffles or an omelet."

Amber throws me a sidelong glance before retorting. "Have what you want! Gary doesn't get to decide for you. You can cook, can't you?"

Beth fidgets uncomfortably in her seat. "It's just that Gary's very particular about my health."

I unroll my napkin and place it on my lap, silently evaluating what I'm hearing. Beth told me she isn't taking any prescription medicine, yet she's clearly out of it at times. Could Gary be putting something in these smoothies he insists she drinks? It sounds unbelievable, but it's not like that kind of stuff never happens. The possibility worries me. Beth has no one to look out for her. She's new to Santa Morelos and doesn't know anyone — she's completely at her husband's mercy. Is that the real reason Gary brought her here for a "fresh start" as he put it, so he could paint a narrative no one could contradict? But what motive could he possibly have for drugging his wife and passing her off as an addict? A cold sweat breaks out on the back of my neck. Is he planning on killing her and counting on it being ruled an overdose?

"How long have you two known each other?" Beth asks, once we've placed our orders.

"Going on fifteen years," Amber answers. "Hard to believe it's been that long. I moved in a few doors down from Kay and we've been best friends ever since. Kay is godmother to my two boys. They're grown now, nineteen and twenty-one, both off at college."

Beth reaches for her water with a shaking hand but doesn't lift it to her lips. Instead, she stares at the glass as though mesmerized by the liquid sloshing back and forth. "I . . . lost my daughter when she was nineteen."

Amber shoots me a panicked look. I warned her not to bring up the topic of Luna — she knows what's at stake. "I'm so sorry, Beth," she says in a subdued tone.

Beth pulls a tissue from her pocket and blows her nose. "I don't like to talk about it." She stands abruptly and reaches for her purse. "Excuse me. I'll be right back."

She trips her way across the restaurant to the restroom, dabbing at her eyes as she goes.

I tent my fingers over my mouth and nose, sick to my stomach. This is not how I envisioned our lunch date going. I was shooting for a light-hearted get-together in the hopes of cheering Beth up and making her feel like she had some friends she could reach out to. "Do you think I should follow her?" I whisper to Amber.

She shakes her head, looking as miserable as I feel. "Give her a few minutes to compose herself. I'm really sorry. I didn't mean to trigger her."

"It's not your fault. She's the one who broached the subject." I throw a quick glance over my shoulder. "I'm not supposed to say this, but Gary told me she's on medication for depression. She has a history of abusing prescription pills and alcohol. That's why her daughter left. She couldn't handle Beth's refusal to get help. But the weird thing is, Beth told me she's not on any medication." I lean forward in my seat and lower my voice. "I'm wondering about those smoothies Gary makes her every morning. What if he's drugging her?"

The server brings our food to the table, and we wait until he waltzes off again before continuing our conversation.

"That's a pretty serious allegation," Amber says, stabbing at her salad. "You'd better be careful about voicing that without any evidence to back it up."

"It wouldn't be hard to prove. All I need to do is get my hands on one of those smoothies he makes her."

"How do you propose doing that?"

"I'm not sure. Maybe I can pretend to be interested in the recipe and ask her to save some in a paper cup for me to try. Then I'll have it tested."

Amber makes a scoffing sound. "If you're right about what's going on, Gary will never let—"

Our heads jerk up in unison at a commotion on the other side of the restaurant. A flustered teenage girl is standing in the hallway to the restrooms talking animatedly with one of the servers. I lock eyes with Amber and jump to my feet, my heart racing. "I'd better make sure Beth's okay."

By the time I cross the restaurant, the manager has been called over. She steps into my path as I attempt to enter the restroom hallway. "I'm sorry, ma'am. The women's restrooms are temporarily closed."

My pulse pounds in my temples. "Why? What's going on?"

"A woman passed out in one of the stalls," she replies. "We've called 911."

"My mom's in there with her," the wide-eyed teenager pipes up. "She's a nurse."

"It's my neighbor. I need to check on her," I say in an urgent tone. "She's here with me and another friend."

The manager eyes me dubiously, not budging from my path.

I point across the restaurant to our table. "We're sitting over there."

The manager tightens her lips. "Give me a minute. I'll check on your neighbor for you." She takes off down the hallway in the direction of the restroom.

I don't wait for permission. I barge through the swing door after her, coming to a sudden halt at the sight that awaits me.

CHAPTER 9

Beth is sprawled on the tile floor, one foot in a bathroom stall, the contents of her purse scattered around her like debris in the aftermath of an explosion. At first glance, I can count at least seven prescription bottles, but there could be more lying in the rubble of make-up, tissues, nail files, hand sanitizer, and hair accessories. My thoughts spin in wild abandon, as I try to make sense of the pattern of destruction. Did she overdose — swallow a bunch of pills? What other explanation could there be? Fear blisters over my skin when I recall Gary's words: *If anything happens to her, I'll hold you accountable.*

A middle-aged, dark-haired woman is leaning over Beth talking to her in the hypnotic, unruffled tone of a professional medic. "That's right, honey, just breathe slowly in and out. You're doing great."

"Wh . . . What happened?" Beth mumbles, brushing a shaky hand over her forehead.

"You fainted, that's all," the woman responds. "You're in the restroom at Trattoria Giuseppe."

Relief surges through me, spurring me into action. "I'm her friend," I say, crouching down next to her. "Beth, it's me, Kay. Are you all right?"

She blinks at me, perplexed. "Who are you?"

The dark-haired woman draws her brows together and eyes me sharply.

"Beth's my neighbor," I explain. "We drove here together."

The woman's face relaxes. "I think she might have hit her head. She needs to get checked out at the hospital. The ambulance is on its way. Maybe you can gather up her stuff."

I give a mute nod and begin shoving random items back into Beth's purse. Oddly enough, I don't see a wallet anywhere. Did she misplace that this morning as well as her phone? Or does Gary forbid her to carry even a meager amount of cash for sundries? I shudder at the thought.

Minutes later, paramedics descend on the scene and whisk Beth off in an ambulance. I retreat to my table, my insides churning. How am I going to break this news to Gary?

"What happened?" Amber asks in an urgent whisper. "The manager wouldn't let me anywhere near the restroom."

"Beth fainted," I say, reaching for my purse. "I need to go to the hospital and find out how she's doing. She didn't recognize me when she came around. She might have a concussion." I fish some cash from my wallet and toss it onto the table next to my plate of barely touched food.

Amber pushes her half-eaten salad aside and gets to her feet. "Do you want me to go with you?"

"No. Go home. I'll fill you in as soon as I know anything."

"Are you going to call Gary?"

I grimace. "I'll have to. He's going to go ballistic. He took a lot of convincing to let me take Beth to lunch to begin with."

"How about I call him for you?" Amber suggests. "That way you can concentrate on getting to the hospital and making sure Beth is okay."

Relief floods through me at the thought of avoiding any interaction with Gary right now. It will be bad enough having to deal with him when he shows up at the ER. "Are you sure?"

"Positive. What's his number?"

I read it off to her, then hurry out to my car. On the way to the hospital, I play the whole scenario back in my head. Beth was clearly upset when she went to the bathroom. Did she take some pills inside one of the stalls? I barely had a chance to glance at the labels on the prescription bottles, and I didn't recognize the ones I saw — but that doesn't mean anything. I'm not on any medication myself so I'm not exactly an expert in these matters. Does Gary even know what she's on? I should have taken a photo of the bottles. But surely the hospital will look into it and ask her about any prescriptions she's taking. Maybe she'll finally get the help she needs.

At the ER reception desk, I give my name and take a seat in the sterile waiting room. Twenty minutes go by before Gary comes storming through the automatic entry doors. He catches sight of me almost instantly and his countenance darkens as he strides over. "I knew I shouldn't have trusted you. What happened?" he snaps.

"Calm down, Gary. Beth fainted in the restroom at the restaurant. They've taken her for a CAT scan. They're concerned she might have a concussion."

He clenches and unclenches his fists, as though sizing me up for a fight. "I told you taking her to lunch was a bad idea. She doesn't function well outside of the house."

I'm tempted to point out that she seemed to be functioning just fine at the block party, but he's already so wound up that I don't want to aggravate the situation.

"Kay Mellows?"

I jump to my feet at the sound of my name. The nurse smiling at me from across the waiting room barely looks old enough to have graduated nursing school. "You can come through and see your friend now."

"That won't be necessary," Gary says, elbowing past me. "It's her fault my wife was brought here in the first place. I'm Gary Finkel, Beth's husband."

The nurse blinks at me questioningly. I repress the sudden urge to explain myself — *I'm not to blame for Beth's problems, her husband is* — but what does the nurse care where the truth lies? She's a disinterested party, just working her shift. I give her a reluctant nod. "That's fine. I'll wait here."

Gary scowls at me again before following the nurse through the double doors into the ER ward. I sink back down on the hard, plastic chair and try to ignore the couple sitting in the corner staring at me with a whole lot less sympathy than before. By the looks on their faces, they've fully bought into Gary's claim that I'm responsible for whatever it is that happened to his wife.

A few minutes later, the nurse reappears. She walks over to me and lowers her voice, an apologetic look on her fresh, young face. "I'm so sorry, but Mr. Finkel is requesting that you leave."

"What? But . . . I just want to know how Beth's doing, that's all."

"She's going to be fine. She has a mild concussion." The nurse clears her throat quietly. "Mr. Finkel has stated that he's afraid for his wife's safety as long as you remain on the premises. If you don't leave voluntarily, he's requested that we have you escorted out of the facility."

CHAPTER 10

I can barely contain my fury on the drive home from the hospital. How dare Gary imply that I'm somehow a danger to Beth. I felt like a criminal walking out of the ER under the accusatory gaze of an overweight security guard as he tapped his fat fingers on the counter he was stationed behind.

Gary's hostile behavior has further convinced me that he's up to something. I can't help but consider the possibility that he set me up. Did he put a little extra something in Beth's smoothie this morning, knowing she was going out to lunch with me? After all, he warned me it would be on my head if anything happened to her — which struck me as an ominous thing to say at the time. Or maybe he was hoping that whatever he dosed Beth with would knock her out before I picked her up and prevent the lunch date from ever taking place. Despite his heartfelt sharing of Beth's struggles, I don't trust him. Am I way off base, or is there something to the nagging feeling in my gut that Gary is orchestrating all of this?

If he's drugging Beth, it would explain why she's so absent-minded all the time. I frown as I pull into my driveway and switch off the engine. But would the drugs really make her do something as goofy as putting her iPad in the fridge or deleting all of her contacts? Gary could be gaslighting her — moving things around to confuse her, messing with her phone. She didn't seem to think she was on any medication, yet multiple different prescription bottles fell out of her purse. Did Gary put them there, or is Beth completely disconnected from reality?

Back inside my house, I call Amber and fill her in on what happened at the hospital.

"Gary was a total jerk," I fume. "He practically had me kicked out of the ER. He even had the gall to tell the staff he was afraid for his wife's safety with me on the premises."

"That's wild!" Amber says. "Oddly enough, he didn't sound angry at all when I called him to let him know Beth had passed out. Just thanked me and said he'd head straight to the hospital."

I let out a *humph*. "I don't trust him. He's a master manipulator. I don't know what his endgame is, but I intend to find out. I'm going to head over to his house the minute he gets back from the hospital and hit him up about his behavior."

"Please don't do anything that stupid! If he's as unpredictable as you say he is, it would be dangerous to engage him. At least wait until Warren gets home and talk it over with him first. Listen, I've got a call coming in. Gotta run. Keep me posted."

Amber hangs up, and I sink down in front of my computer to try to catch up on my work. But even as my fingers fly over the keys, my mind continually wanders next door as I try to psychoanalyze our new neighbors and work out who the real victim is. Is Beth at the mercy of a controlling husband, or is Gary the long-suffering spouse of a lying, thieving addict?

The minute Warren arrives home from work, I recount what happened and add my unsolicited commentary. "Gary was unbelievably rude and unappreciative. He made me feel like a heel. He's a very unpleasant person. I'm not even sure I want him living next door anymore."

"I agree he overreacted," Warren says, his tone cautious as he sinks down on the couch in front of the television. "But you need to cut him some slack. He was probably worried sick about his wife."

"*I'm* worried about her," I shoot back. "I think Gary might be drugging her. She told us he makes her a smoothie every morning before he goes to work, and he insists she drinks it in front of him before he leaves. What does that tell you?"

Warren eyes me warily, as though trying to gauge if he can safely reason with me. "Not a whole lot, to be honest. I make you coffee every morning, don't I? Maybe Gary's just trying to be a good husband."

"I'm not buying it. I'm not convinced he's acting in her best interests. She might be in danger."

Warren sets down the TV remote he's holding, his brow crumpling. "It doesn't do any good to speculate. I know how you and Amber get to talking. Next thing you know all sorts of rumors will be flying back and forth among the neighbors."

I quirk an eyebrow. "Which is why I need evidence to support my suspicions."

"Kay, please—"

I hold up a hand. "Don't say it!"

Warren blinks at me, an injured expression on his face. "Say what?"

"Whatever it is you were going to say. I'm going to get to the bottom of what's going on next door, and nothing will dissuade me."

I turn on my heel and stomp outside to wheel the trash can to the curb. I need some fresh air to clear my pounding head and the smell of antiseptic that still lingers in my nostrils. After trundling the can down the driveway, I spot a white trash bag lying next to the curb. It looks like a dog might have been tearing at it. I tut my disapproval as I make my way over to grab it. It must belong to Gary — his can is overflowing. I'll have to have a word with him about leaving trash bags at the curb. It's strictly against HOA rules.

I'm about to toss the bag into my garbage can when I notice an ivory strap protruding through it. My heart begins to beat like a tribal drum. I shoot a glance at Gary and Beth's house but the curtains are tightly drawn. Kneeling down, I peer inside the trash bag, confirming my initial suspicion.

CHAPTER 11

The hair on the back of my neck prickles as I pull the purse from the trash bag and examine it. Ivory with a gold zipper. It matches the description of Maria's purse. It can't be a coincidence. I don't see any obvious damage or tears — no good reason why someone would have thrown it in the trash, unless they were trying to hide it.

Tucking the purse under my arm, I hurry around to the back of my house out of view of my neighbors and my husband. With shaking hands, I unzip the purse and retrieve the wallet inside. It comes as no real surprise that Maria Torres is the name on the driver's license, but it leaves me reeling with shock, nonetheless. We have a thief in our midst — one that I welcomed into the neighborhood. It's a devastating blow. I've worked hard to build a community that supports and trusts one another. This feels like the worst kind of betrayal.

I grimace as I flick through the contents of the wallet. The cash is gone, but Maria's cards are still there. I feel sick to my stomach. Beth has been lying to me — hiding her addiction. And Gary covered up what she did. He's the one who takes out the trash — he must have known Maria's purse was in the bag. It's such a shame that a sweet old lady, who would give her last dollar to anyone who asked, has been ripped off like this.

Despite what Beth has done, I can't help but feel sorry for her. She must have been desperate to steal from her elderly neighbor. Gary has essentially cut her off from the outside world. She has no independence left. Her only hope of getting her hands on any money, or drugs to numb her pain, is by doing exactly what she did.

My mind spins as I mull over what to do about the situation. If there was some way to resolve it without involving the police, I would be all over it. On the other hand, turning Beth in might get her the help she needs. It's not as if she's getting much help from Gary, as far as I can tell. If my hunch is right, he's keeping her in a weakened, confused state for his own nefarious purpose, which I have yet to figure out. I pull my sweater tight around me, shivering in the evening chill. I need to find a way to return Maria's purse to her without divulging where I found it.

"Hey! What are you doing?"

I startle at the sound of Warren's voice. He's standing in the back door holding a mug aloft. "I made us some hot chocolate. Come inside. It's freezing out here."

"Be right there," I call back, darting a quick glance around to see if there's anywhere nearby I can hide the purse. "I was just taking the trash out."

Warren frowns. "What's that under your arm?"

I tense, then put a finger to my lips and shoo him back into the kitchen. Maybe it's better if Warren knows what's going on next door. I only hope I can persuade him not to turn Beth in. "I'll explain inside. I don't want to talk about it out here."

He raises his brows but turns around without another word and disappears inside. I take a moment to compose myself, then follow him into the house and set the purse down on the kitchen island. "It's Maria's missing purse," I say quietly.

"What?" Warren's eyes widen. "Where did you find it?"

I let a significant pause ensue before answering. "In our neighbors' trash." I don't actually know if the bag was the Finkels' trash, but it's close enough to the truth. Who else would have dumped it at the curb?

Warren blinks, a befuddled look on his face. "You mean . . . our renters?"

"That's exactly who I'm talking about."

Warren sinks down on a bar stool, a wary look in his eyes. "Were you going through their trash or something?"

"Of course not," I snap. "Their can was overflowing, and they left a plastic bag lying out at the curb. It looked like an animal might have gotten into it, so I picked it up to toss it into our can. That's when I noticed the strap sticking out through a hole in the bag. I knew Maria's missing purse was ivory colored, so I decided to take a closer look. My hunch was right. Her driver's license is in the wallet. The cash is gone — eighty dollars in total — but everything else is still there."

Warren creases his brow. "It doesn't make sense. Why would someone steal a purse and not keep the credit cards?"

I let out a sigh. "I didn't want to have to tell you this, but Beth has a prescription pill addiction. Gary says she's been caught shoplifting before." I leave out any mention of possible alcohol abuse. It might be enough to push Warren over the edge and insist on evicting them.

He rubs the stubble on his jaw, looking shaken at the news. "Are you going to notify the police?"

"I can't ignore the fact that a crime was committed. But first, I'm going to confront our neighbors and see what they have to say for themselves. Maybe we can resolve this with a contrite apology and restitution."

"I don't know if that's such a good idea after everything you told me about Gary's reaction at the hospital."

"If I can resolve this without involving the authorities, it will be better for everyone. I should at least give Beth the chance to come clean about what she did and apologize."

Warren grunts. "That's awfully optimistic."

I reach for my mug of hot chocolate and take a sip, savoring the sweet warmth it offers to my chilled innards. "It's worth a try. I'll go over there and have a conversation with them at least. I need to clear the air after what happened at the hospital anyway."

Warren grimaces. "Not alone, you're not. I'll go with you."

"I don't need protection. Gary's hardly going to attack me at his front door."

Warren puckers his brow. "I just think it would be best to have a witness to what's said, in case things go south."

"Fine. In that case, let's go talk to them right now," I say, slinging the strap of Maria's purse over my shoulder. "No time like the present."

Warren rings the doorbell and we wait on the front steps in a taut silence. I'm still trying to wrap my head around how Maria's purse ended up in the trash. Was Gary trying to cover up what his wife had done, or did Beth manage to discard it without his knowledge?

Gary opens the door to us, a scowl immediately clouding his face. "Beth's not in any state to see you, if that's why you're here."

"Actually, it's you I wanted to talk to," I say, fighting to keep my expression neutral. "Can we come in? It's important."

He hesitates, his gaze flicking between Warren and me. "If you insist, but keep it down. Beth's trying to sleep." He turns abruptly and leads the way to the kitchen, where he leans back against the counter, arms folded in front of him. He's already got his defenses up, as though he's expecting me to lay into him about his attitude in the ER.

I set Maria's purse down on the kitchen table in full view of him, but he doesn't react. Does he recognize it? If he's bluffing, he's doing a good job. He doesn't offer us a seat, but I pull out a chair and sit down anyway.

"How's Beth doing?" Warren asks.

"She's pretty shaken up and confused about what happened." Gary shoots me an aggrieved look. "I shouldn't have agreed to let you take her to lunch. I knew it would prove too much for her."

I bristle at his reprimanding tone, insinuating that I'm responsible for his wife's condition. I still haven't ruled out the possibility that he set me up by doping her before she left the house. "I noticed Beth had several prescription bottles in her purse," I say. "I'm worried she might be over-medicating." I hold Gary's gaze, but he doesn't flinch under my unrelenting stare.

Instead, he lets out a scoffing laugh. "Not a chance. I fill those bottles of hers with placebo pills I buy on Amazon. With her history, I can't trust her. I control her actual prescriptions. There's no possible way for her to self-medicate."

"Not unless she has access to cash." I reach for the purse and hold it up to him. "I found Maria's missing purse in a plastic bag near your trash can. All the cash is gone."

Gary frowns at the purse, then glares at me. "What exactly are you implying?"

"I'm not *implying* anything. I'm stating a fact. You must have known the purse was in the trash bag. Are you trying to cover up what Beth did?"

A deep flush spreads up Gary's neck. "If you're accusing my wife of stealing our neighbor's purse, you're barking up the wrong tree. Just because I shared some personal information with you about what happened in the past, it doesn't give you the right to jump to vile conclusions. Someone else must have tossed that trash bag by our can to pin the blame on us. Beth couldn't have stolen Maria's purse. She was with me the entire time the day of the block party."

Gary takes a leaden step toward me, his breathing labored. "You know what I think? Someone's trying to set my wife up, and it better not be you!"

CHAPTER 12

It's been three days since Warren and I went over to speak to Gary about finding Maria's missing purse in the trash. He was adamant that neither he nor Beth knew anything about it. He even floated the possibility that I was trying to frame them. He accused me of spreading unwarranted rumors in the neighborhood about him and Beth, and made it clear he regretted confiding in me.

It's true that I've expressed some of my concerns about the Finkels to Warren, and Amber, and Maria, and maybe a couple of the other neighbors, but I wouldn't call it *spreading rumors* per se. I tried to reassure Gary that I only ever wanted to befriend Beth, not hurt her by using what he told me against her. But the conversation only deteriorated from that point on, and he ended up asking Warren and me to leave.

That was twice in one day he kicked me out, and I never even got a chance to address his inappropriate behavior toward me at the hospital. It's too late now to bring it up, but I haven't forgotten how he twisted the situation to make me look like the bad guy. He's proving to be a masterful gaslighter. No wonder Beth feels so hopeless about her situation. I have to find a way to help her.

After thinking the situation over, I replace the eighty dollars in Maria's purse myself and return it to her, telling her that the UPS guy found it in some bushes. When I suggest that maybe it inadvertently got picked up in the scavenger hunt, she seems satisfied by the explanation. No one wants to believe there's a thief living among us.

This morning I'm taking some freshly baked muffins next door to check up on Beth. I'm growing increasingly worried by the fact that I still haven't laid eyes on her since she got back from the hospital. I told Gary he shouldn't leave her alone all day while she's recovering from a concussion, but he's been taking off early for work every morning as usual.

I decide it might be best to avoid the front door camera this time and go around to the back instead — I'd rather not alert Gary to my visit. I knock on the kitchen window, but Beth doesn't answer. There's no sign of her inside, so I try the back door handle. To my surprise, it's unlocked.

"Beth?" I call out, stepping inside. "Are you home?"

I hear a scuffling sound and, moments later, she shuffles into the kitchen belting her robe around her waist. I'm shocked by her gaunt appearance. She's lost weight in the days since our lunch date, and her face is pale — sunken hollows framing her sad eyes. She looks like she hasn't slept in days. "What . . . are you doing here?" she asks, rubbing frantically at a patch on her forehead.

"I just wanted to pop over and see how you're feeling," I reply, forcing a cheerful grin, when what I really want to do is take her in my arms and hug her bony frame and whisk her out of here. "I brought you some homemade muffins."

Her gaze zigzags from the muffins to the door, then back to me. "Gary doesn't want you coming over here."

I let out an exasperated sigh. "Beth, you don't have to stand for that nonsense. He doesn't own you."

She sinks down in a chair at the kitchen table. "He's just looking out for me. I can't be trusted." She cocks her head to one side as though considering the validity of what she's said. "No, I definitely can't be trusted. I'm a terrible person."

A prickle goes up my spine. What is she alluding to? Is she going to own up to stealing Maria's purse? "What do you mean, you can't be trusted?"

She flaps a hand at me, her thin wrist looking as though it can barely support its own weight. "I keep doing stupid things — awful things. And then I don't remember what I've done. I'm a danger to myself and others."

"You mean like putting your iPad in the fridge?"

She jerks her head in my direction. "You know about that?"

"You told me," I remind her gently. "Don't you remember?"

She shrugs. "I can't remember half of what I say or do. Every day there's something new. Just yesterday, I opened the mail and threw away some important stuff. Credit card bills and the like. Gary was furious with me. I don't know what I was thinking." She looks at me with the same pleading look that was in her eyes the first time I met her. "Do you think I'm crazy?"

I take a silent breath before replying. I don't want to come across too strong, like Warren always says I do, but this is my chance to gain her trust. This is as close as she's come to asking me for help.

I lean toward her and quiet my voice. "Beth, do you think there's a possibility that Gary's doing some of these things to make you think you're crazy?"

CHAPTER 13

Beth looks at me blankly. "Gary would never . . . I mean . . ." Her voice trails off and she drops her gaze, frowning at the hardwood floor as though, for the first time, seriously considering the prospect that her husband might be gaslighting her. I could prove it to her by telling her about the placebo pills Gary admitted to filling her prescription bottles with, but that might backfire. If Beth really is struggling with addiction, it's better she remains unaware that she's swallowing a harmless substitute. By all appearances, the alcohol is enough of a problem for her to wrestle with.

I throw a quick glance around the kitchen, but I don't see any vodka sitting out on the counter this time. Instead, my eyes land on a hard plastic tumbler with the remnants of a green drink inside. The hairs on my arms stand to attention. If this is the smoothie Gary makes her each morning, this could be my chance to test my theory. "How about I make us some coffee to go with the muffins?" I suggest, jumping to my feet before Beth can protest.

She picks nervously at her sleeve. "You're not supposed to be here. What if Gary FaceTimes me? He likes to check up on what I'm doing."

"If he does, I'll slip out the back door, so you don't have to lie to him." I reach for the tumbler and wave it in her direction. "This looks yummy. Is this the shake you were telling me about?"

She frowns, as though trying to remember when we had that conversation.

"I've been meaning to ask you for the recipe," I go on, lifting two mugs down from the open shelf above the coffeemaker.

"I think it's . . . mango . . . spinach, and flaxseed. Maybe some protein powder too," she says, sounding groggy. "At least I think that's what Gary said the powdery stuff was. My memory's not the best these days."

Her eyelids flutter as though she's on the verge of sleep. I need to get some coffee in her as quickly as possible.

"No worries," I say nonchalantly. "I'll ask him for the recipe next time I see him." I open and close a couple of drawers pretending to look for a teaspoon, while discreetly pulling out a quart-sized Ziploc bag. Hunched over the sink, I hurriedly scrape the remnants of the smoothie into it and slip it into my pocket. I make a show of rinsing out the tumbler and loading it in the dishwasher before turning my attention back to making our coffee. My heart is thudding in triple time. I only hope Beth can't hear it over the gurgling of the coffeemaker. I can scarcely believe I pulled off getting a sample of her smoothie so easily after all. Now, I just need to figure out where to take it to have it tested.

I set a mug of steaming coffee in front of Beth. "Cream and sugar?"

She gives a jerky shake of her head. "I'm not allowed sugar or processed foods. Gary says they're bad for me. They affect my moods."

I shove the plate of muffins toward her. "My rules are a little different. There's nothing more healing to the soul than a freshly baked muffin."

Beth eyes the plate longingly, swallowing down her reluctance to break the rules as she slowly reaches a frail hand out

53

for a muffin. I watch with a conflicting mix of horror and satisfaction as she devours it like a famished child. Has Gary been rationing her food — or worse, starving her — since she got out of the hospital? My stomach churns at the thought. My resolve to do something to help her only strengthens as I watch her gobble down a second muffin.

As soon as I leave here, I'll turn in that sample to the police station and explain my concerns to them. Warren won't approve if he finds out what I'm up to, but I've got to trust my instincts. Whatever Beth's vices are, it's obvious she's a hapless victim in an abusive relationship. She needs an advocate, and I'm the only one she's got.

CHAPTER 14

On the way to the station, I go over in my mind what I need to say to convince the police to take Beth's situation seriously. They're going to be skeptical, of course, but once I tell them everything I've observed, they'll be obligated to do a welfare check at a minimum. Hopefully, they can keep my name out of it. It would be better if Gary doesn't know that I'm the one who instigated the investigation, but I'm not sure how that works from a legal standpoint. I'm going ahead with it regardless, because it's the right thing to do. Something is very wrong next door, and I would feel awful if anything happened to Beth and I hadn't at least tried to get her the help she so desperately needs.

Inside the station, I'm relegated to a wobbly, plastic chair to wait for an available officer, which the indifferent desk clerk tells me could be a while as I have neither an appointment nor an emergency. I could have argued the point, as no one knows how critical the situation really is — Beth could be dead by the time I get back to the house, for that matter. But I don't want to start things off on the wrong foot, so I dutifully take a seat and wait as directed.

"Mrs. Mellows?"

I scramble out of my thoughts and jump to my feet to greet the vaguely familiar, imposing officer stretching a hairy hand toward me. "I'm Officer Engelmann," he says, dipping his head in greeting.

"Call me Kay, please," I say, following him down the corridor and into a stuffy office.

"I believe we've met before," Engelmann says, eying me with an air of amusement as I take the seat he proffers me. "Right around Thanksgiving last year, wasn't it?"

"Um, yes, that's right." I grimace inwardly when I think back to the awkward encounter. I called the police to report a burglary at the Wades' house, only to find out that Tom Wade had locked himself out and was climbing in a window. I should have recognized him, but to be fair, it was dark, and I didn't have my glasses on. A rush to judgement, to be sure. But as president of the HOA, I hadn't wanted to appear derelict in my duties. It was shortly after that I purchased the binoculars to safeguard against any future embarrassing misunderstandings.

"What can I do for you today, Kay?" Engelmann asks, settling into his swivel chair and smoothing a finger over his thick, black mustache. His eyes flick pointedly over the files stacked on his desk, not so subtly conveying that he has better things to do than entertain my neighborhood grievances. But that's not why I'm here. I need to put him straight, and quickly.

I pull out the Ziploc bag and set it on the desk between us. "In a nutshell, I think my neighbor is being drugged by her husband."

Engelmann's eyebrows twitch upward, the only hint that my opening has grabbed his attention. He reaches for the plastic bag and peers at the treacly, green contents as though trying to decipher the ingredients.

"It's the remnants of a smoothie her husband makes her every morning," I say. "He always insists that she drinks it before he leaves for work. It makes her groggy and out of it. He also told me she has a problem with prescription pills and that he's been filling her medication bottles with placebos. I don't know whether to believe him or not. He could be over-medicating her, for all I know. He gaslights her all the time about stuff. I've tried to befriend her, hoping she'll open up to me, but I think she's scared to say anything, or maybe she doesn't entirely grasp what's happening."

Engelmann sets the Ziploc down, his face an expressionless mask.

"Can you have the contents tested?" I ask. "I'm afraid for my neighbor's safety."

Engelmann leans his elbows on the desk and interlocks his fingers. "I appreciate your concern for your neighbor's well-being, but that isn't how this works. We can't just randomly test samples of undetermined origin that someone brings us. If a crime is suspected, we have to collect our own evidence on site, and we can't do that without probable cause."

"But I'm telling you there is probable cause. My neighbor's husband is extremely controlling. He never lets her leave the house on her own. He's constantly moving things around and throwing stuff away, and blaming her for it. He even took away her car keys when . . ." I break off, not wanting to throw Beth under the bus for a DUI.

"You were saying," Engelmann prods.

"She, uh, she had a problem with alcohol in the past."

He gives a thoughtful nod. "In that case, I commend her husband for doing the responsible thing. Do you know if your neighbor's still drinking? That might explain why she seems out of it."

The half-empty vodka bottle flashes to mind, but I push the thought away. I have no evidence it was Beth who drank it. It could have been Gary, or perhaps he left it there to make her think she'd been drinking again.

"I don't believe so," I say, a tad defensively. "I've never seen her touch alcohol."

Engelmann pushes the Ziploc bag back across the desk to me. "My advice is to keep reaching out to your neighbor — let her know you're there if she needs you. Like it or not, there's nothing illegal about being a controlling jerk of a husband. Unless you actually witness some kind of abuse, there's nothing I can do to help."

CHAPTER 15

I sip my double shot of espresso as I log on to my computer to tackle my email backlog. I haven't checked up on Beth in several days, as I haven't been feeling all that well myself. I dropped the smoothie sample off at an independent lab to be tested, and I've been having crazy nightmares and losing sleep ever since. Warren says it's because I'm obsessing too much about the situation next door — imagining the worst when there might be a simple explanation. He wouldn't approve of me wasting money to have the smoothie sample tested, so I'm not going to mention it to him unless it comes back positive. I know he's worried about me. He even suggested going away this weekend for a change of scene, but I'm reluctant to leave Beth — I'd never forgive myself if something happened to her while we were gone.

I'm upset that Officer Engelmann didn't take my concerns more seriously. He didn't even think they merited a welfare check when I pressed the point. Waiting until I witness some kind of abuse before acting on it is as dumb as telling someone who's being stalked to wait until they've been attacked before reporting it. Everyone seems to think I'm overreacting — everyone except Amber. She saw firsthand what happened at Trattoria Giuseppe. She agrees there might be something to my theory that my neighbor is being drugged. Maybe I can ask her to check up on Beth for me today.

I set down my mug and reach for my phone.

"Hey, I was just thinking about you," Amber says. "How are you feeling? Do you need anything — groceries, errands, whatever?"

"No, we're good, thanks. Warren stopped by the store yesterday on his way home from work. I think I'm rallying, although I still feel exhausted, but I do have a favor to ask. Do you have time to check up on Beth today? I don't feel up to going over there myself, but someone should look in on her — see if she needs anything."

"Of course, no problem. I'll stop by right now, and then pop in and give you a report."

"Don't go to the front door. Gary's got that camera rigged up, and Beth won't answer the doorbell anyway. Go around to the back. It's usually unlocked."

I down the rest of my espresso while I watch for Amber to arrive. True to her word, she shows up ten minutes later and walks around to the back of the rental. When she doesn't reappear, I take it she's gotten inside. Hopefully, Beth's not too out of it and remembers who Amber is. The last thing I need is for her to make a frantic 911 call to report a stranger in her house. Gary would blow a fuse, and he might even threaten Amber with a restraining order. I would have to admit to instigating the visit, and I sense Officer Engelmann's patience is wearing thin with me.

I thought about telling him that Maria's purse had shown up in a trash bag at the curb, but I didn't think he'd be too receptive to my theory that Gary put it there — not without evidence. But I can't imagine how else Maria's purse could have ended up there. I thought about confronting Beth to see what she has to say about it, but I'm not sure she'd remember if she'd done it anyway. In her current state, it seems a stretch to think that she's capable of going into someone's house and

59

stealing a purse. Gary might have stolen it to frame her. He might even have fed me the shoplifting story to paint her in a bad light, and left the purse out by the trash hoping I would report it to the police and have Beth prosecuted. My skin tingles at the thought. If I'm right, he's not just a domineering jerk, he's a sociopath who takes delight in tormenting his wife.

I hear a knock at the back door and get up to answer it.

"You look terrible," Amber says, breezing past me and tossing her keys on the table.

"I've barely slept for the past three nights," I say, sinking back down in my chair. "I've been having the worst nightmares."

"About what?" Amber asks, helping herself to a coffee.

"Weird, macabre stuff. Gary peeling off a mask and revealing that he's really a monster underneath. Finding Beth dead at her kitchen table with a smoothie mustache. It all feels so real in the moment. I'm scared to fall asleep now, which isn't helping with the sleep deprivation."

Amber sinks down next to me at the table and peers at me over the rim of her mug. "That doesn't sound like our indomitable HOA president, dispenser of good will and happy thoughts."

"Very funny." I pull my hair back from my face and twist it into a knot at the nape of my neck. That small effort is all the grooming I've done today. I just don't have the energy to care what I look like after tossing and turning all night long. "How's my neighbor?"

Amber sips her coffee. "Apparently, she has the flu, which is why she hasn't been up and around for a few days."

I rumple my brow in confusion. "What do you mean *apparently*?"

"I didn't see her. I spoke with Gary. He told me he came home early to look after her."

My chest tightens. I don't believe for one minute that he's capable of such an unselfish act. "So, you didn't actually *see* Beth. Did you hear her moving around at all? Or did you hear her talking to Gary?"

Amber shakes her head, her fingers coiled tightly around her mug. "Nope. He said she was asleep."

A chill ripples down my back. "I don't like the sound of that."

Amber raises an inquisitive brow. "What do you mean?"

"What do you think I mean? Gary's a snake. We can't trust anything he tells us. He's essentially been keeping Beth a prisoner in her own house." I hesitate, sucking on my bottom lip. "He could have killed her, for all anyone knows."

CHAPTER 16

By the following morning, I feel marginally better, so I decide to make some chicken noodle soup and take it next door to Beth. I should probably stick to vegetable soup in case Gary finds out about it, but it's not nourishing enough if she really does have the flu — which I'm skeptical of. I want to make sure to get over there and back before noon in case Gary returns home from work early again. I've just finished chopping up the vegetables and tossing everything into the cast-iron pot on the stove when my doorbell rings. I answer it to find Maria Torres standing on the steps.

"Good morning, Kay," she says. "I brought you some homemade cookies as a thank you for finding my purse."

"That's very thoughtful of you, but you really didn't have to do that. Come on in," I say, ushering her inside. "Can I get you a cup of coffee or tea?"

She grunts as she settles into a chair at the kitchen table. "A cup of tea with a drop of milk would be lovely, thank you."

"Coming right up."

"Something smells good in here," Maria says, glancing over at the pot on the stove.

"It's chicken noodle soup. I'm making it for Beth. She has the flu."

"The flu?" Maria echoes in a surprised tone. "When did she come down with it?"

"A few days ago. She's been in bed ever since, poor thing."

Maria blinks at me, the papery folds of her skin pleating in confusion. "She seemed fine when I saw her last night."

I freeze, one hand on the refrigerator door. "You . . . saw Beth Finkel last night?"

"Yes. She and Gary sometimes walk late at night. I don't sleep all that well in my bed, so I usually sit in my recliner by the family room window. I saw them around midnight walking down the street with flashlights. They looked like they were arguing about something."

I retrieve the milk from the fridge and pour some into a jug, taken aback by what Maria's telling me. It's hard to imagine Beth is alert enough to go out walking late at night — let alone when she's battling the flu. It's a relief to hear that Gary allows her out to get some regular exercise, but it appears he's going to great lengths to keep her from coming in contact with any of the neighbors. Why else would they walk at midnight in the cold?

Maria pours some milk into her tea and stirs it. "I know you worry about Gary bullying his wife, but she can be quite the feisty one herself, from what I observed."

I stare at her in bewilderment. Maybe Maria's mixing Gary and Beth up with some other couple out for a midnight stroll. Her eyesight's not that great, even during daylight hours.

"I wouldn't describe Beth as feisty," I say. "In my experience, she's quite passive, especially around Gary."

Maria purses her lips. "You would have been proud of her the other night — standing up for herself like she did. She was chewing Gary out for something, flailing her arms all around and yelling at him when he shoved her. She put on quite a show."

I almost choke on a mouthful of tea. "Are you sure it was Gary and Beth you saw?"

"Oh, yes! It was definitely the Finkels. They stopped directly under the streetlight outside my house. Gary was checking something on his phone."

I chew thoughtfully on a cookie, savoring the freshly baked taste of cinnamon and brown sugar. The whole scenario sounds peculiar. Maria might have misinterpreted what she saw. I can't picture Beth ever standing up to Gary, but I'm glad to hear she has recovered enough from the flu to go out walking. Maybe now my nightmares about seeing her locked up and starving to death will taper off.

Maria drains her tea and gets to her feet with a grunt. "Well, I should get back to Smokey and Flora. They don't like it when I'm gone too long."

"Thanks for the cookies, Maria. They're delicious."

"Thank *you* for finding my purse." She gives a perplexed shake of her head. "I still can't figure out how those teenagers ever thought it was part of the scavenger hunt. To be honest, I wondered if Gary Finkel might have taken it out of spite. He's always complaining about my cats sleeping in the window and taunting the dog across the street. He says the barking drives him around the bend. I half suspected he might have opened my back door knowing the cats would run away, and taken the purse to fake a break-in. He seems the vindictive type." She sighs. "Too bad we can't trust our neighbors anymore. Or the youth. But these are the times we live in."

I swallow down my guilt at hiding the truth from her. I hate that I cast aspersions on the kids who participated in the scavenger hunt, but it was the best excuse I could come up with at the time. I don't want Beth to be charged when I'm not sure she was responsible for stealing the purse in the first place.

After Maria leaves, I ladle half of the chicken noodle soup into a Tupperware container and add a couple of homemade bread rolls I had in the freezer before heading out to deliver my care package.

I'm surprised to find the back door to Beth's house locked. I knock on the kitchen window several times, but there's no response. I walk around to the front of the house and try the doorbell, beaming at the camera in case Gary is watching. After several more attempts, I return home and replace the soup in the fridge. Beth might be sleeping. I'll try again this afternoon, if Gary isn't back by then.

Despite my exhaustion, I manage to get a few hours of work in before Warren arrives home.

"Is it that time already?" I ask, checking my phone and stretching my arms above my head. I get to my feet and give Warren a hug before heading to the kitchen. "I made chicken noodle soup earlier. I need to take some over to Beth, then I'll heat up the rest for us."

"Sounds good," he replies. "I'm going to jump in the shower."

I grab the Tupperware from the fridge and walk next door for the second time today. Just as I'm about to ring the doorbell, Gary's BMW screeches into the driveway.

I grit my teeth, steeling myself for the showdown that's been percolating ever since he had me escorted out of the hospital.

CHAPTER 17

I paste on the semblance of a smile as Gary climbs out of his car and strides up to me.

"I brought over some homemade chicken noodle soup for Beth," I say. "How's she doing?"

He presses his lips into a disapproving line. "I thought I made it clear you're not welcome here. You're not a good influence on my wife."

"I don't know how you can say that with a straight face," I fire back. "I've gone out of my way to befriend Beth and help her in whatever way I can. You're the one keeping her trapped inside her own house and refusing to let her have a life of her own."

"How Beth and I conduct our lives is none of your business. You're forever trying to stick your nose in our affairs and putting all sorts of crazy ideas about me in my wife's head. If you don't stop harassing us and gossiping about us, I'm going to call the police. All we want is to be left alone. We're not causing any trouble in the neighborhood. We don't play loud music, we don't have people over, and we don't leave our junk lying around in the yard. What more do you want?"

"I want to see Beth," I say, jutting out my chin.

"She's not up for a visit, from you or anyone else."

I arch a scathing eyebrow. "Then how come she was able to go for a walk at midnight last night?"

A flash of anger crosses Gary's face before he quickly masks it. "I don't know what you're talking about."

"Maria Torres saw you and Beth arguing outside her house last night."

He curls his lip in disgust. "You can't believe a word that woman says. She's blind as a bat. She couldn't possibly have seen us, even if we had been out walking that late, which we weren't. I don't know why she has it in for us — spreading ridiculous rumors about us arguing in the middle of the night. The more I think about it, the more I suspect she stashed her purse next to our trash to set us up."

"That's absurd! I've known Maria for years. She wouldn't do something like that. What would be her motive?"

Gary's eyes rake over me scathingly. "She's old, lonely, and desperate for attention. How's that for starters?"

My stomach roils with anger. "You're the one who sounds desperate — desperate to put the blame anywhere than where it should be. We both know Beth took that purse and you covered up what she did. Either that, or you set her up. Look, I don't want to see her prosecuted. I only want to help her. You must realize you're driving her to take these kinds of risks. She has no freedom and no access to any money of her own."

Gary glares at me. "How would you know?"

"I have eyes to see what's going on. She doesn't even carry a wallet. Is that another one of your arbitrary rules? Beth's too scared to stand up to you, but I'm not. I'm not going to let you continue to bully your wife in my rental house!"

Gary lets out a growl and lunges toward me, but I manage to sidestep him. The Tupperware container I was holding goes flying and soup splatters all over the driveway. I hear a loud yell from our doorway, then the steady thud of footsteps. Warren bolts to my side and grabs me, looking me over as though he's afraid something might be broken. "Are you okay?"

I give a jerky nod, too shocked and angry to speak.

Warren wheels around to face Gary. "I saw what you did. You tried to attack my wife."

"You're out of your mind," Gary says, taking a step backward. "I never laid a hand on her."

"Only because she was quick enough to dodge you. What's your problem anyway? All she was doing was being a good neighbor and bringing Beth some soup."

Gary's gaze flits back to me and his shoulders suddenly slump. He lets out a heavy sigh. "Look, I'm sorry. I've been under a lot of stress lately, and I didn't appreciate being confronted in my driveway the minute I stepped out of my car."

"I didn't confront you," I say, prickling with indignation. "I was showing some concern for your sick wife, which is more than you do."

"I don't think chicken noodle soup is going to help Beth," Gary says in a subdued tone.

I want to retort that it's got to be better than those wretched smoothies he forces her to drink, but I manage to bite my tongue.

"Why don't you both come in for a few minutes?" Gary says in a conciliatory tone.

Warren and I exchange a look of surprise at the dramatic turnaround. I'm wondering what the catch is. Maybe Gary's afraid we're going to try and evict him after this latest incident, and he wants to smooth things over. Whatever his motive, it's a chance to see Beth in the flesh and reassure myself that she's okay. "I have some more chicken noodle soup in the fridge," I say. "I'll just run back and fetch—"

"Can we just forget about the soup for now?" Gary interrupts.

Warren lays a hand on my arm and gives a subtle nod, pleading for me to go along with it. We follow Gary inside and I cast a quick glance up the stairs on the off chance that Beth has heard the commotion and come out of her room, but there's no sign of her.

Gary leads us into the family room, and gestures for us to take a seat on the couch. He throws himself down in a chair and drops his head into his hands. A long, uncomfortable silence ensues. I grimace at Warren, and he gives a helpless shrug.

"Gary, don't you want to check on Beth now that you're home?" I ask, when I can take the silence no longer.

He shakes his head. "I can't."

"Why not? I'll go check on her for you," I say, getting to my feet.

He lets out a long, heavy breath. "Don't waste your time. Beth's gone."

CHAPTER 18

For a suspended moment in time, I'm too taken aback to speak. *Beth's gone.* What does that mean exactly? My mind runs through several possibilities. Could she have gone to visit her sister? Gone to the store? Or wandered off in a drugged-up haze? Did she leave Gary? *Of course!* That must be it. That explains why he's so upset and angry. My stomach fizzes with a mixture of excitement and fear for Beth. Does Gary know where she is? I hope he's not planning on going after her. I should call her, offer her some cash and a safe place to stay. Hopefully, she had the gumption to take her phone with her. My eyes dart around the room, searching for any sign of it.

"Where did she go?" Warren asks, interrupting my frenzied thoughts.

Gary rubs a hand over the stubble on his jaw. "She checked into a rehab facility."

I let out a gasp. "What? When did this happen?"

"This morning. We left at 4.00 a.m. I asked for the day off work and took her there myself."

I sink back among the cushions, reeling from the news. I had no idea Beth was thinking about going to rehab. She never even hinted at it. In all of our conversations, she was adamant she wasn't taking any pills or drinking alcohol anymore. But I can't deny that all the signs pointed to it — her slurred speech, poor memory, and shaky gait. "Did she go . . . voluntarily?" I ask.

Gary throws me an irritated look. "Of course she did — not that it's any of your business."

I jerk my chin at him. "I'm her neighbor, her landlord, and her friend. It's only natural I'd be concerned when she disappears from one day to the next. Especially when she's been sick with the flu."

Gary rubs his hands in a sheepish manner. "I only told people she had the flu to get you to stay away. Beth and I have been discussing this in private for several days now, and I wanted it to be her decision. I didn't want anyone else influencing her. I've been stressing out about the fact that she'd relapsed since the move — she's been consuming pills and alcohol behind my back again."

I eye him skeptically. "How is she able to get her hands on alcohol when she never leaves the house?"

"Delivery." Gary lets out a long, shuddering breath. "She was lying when she said she didn't have access to money. She siphons plenty out of our accounts."

"If she's stealing from you, maybe she lied about taking Maria's purse too," Warren interjects.

Gary glares at him, squeezing his hands into fists. "She didn't take it. Only a loser would do something that low."

I squirm in my seat. I need to change the subject before things turn physical. Maybe Gary's in denial about how far Beth was willing to go to feed her habit, but it's irrelevant now that she's checked herself into rehab. "I'm shocked she agreed to get help," I say. "She never mentioned she was considering rehab. Quite the opposite. She didn't seem to think she had a problem."

"She wanted to go," Gary assures me. "But it wasn't an easy decision for her — facing up to the fact that she'd relapsed."

"How long will she be gone?" I ask.

"That's up to her," he replies, bouncing his knee up and down. "She's signed up for a three-month program, but she could be there as long as nine months, if that's what it takes."

I squeeze my hands together in my lap, trying to digest the news. That's a long time to be gone. It seems odd that Beth didn't even hint at what she was planning to do, or make any attempt to say goodbye before she left. Perhaps Gary didn't give her the opportunity. I'm troubled by the feeling that he's not giving us the whole story. Maybe it was his decision — he could have whisked her off in the early hours without her having any prior knowledge of his intentions. Is that even legal? Wouldn't he have to petition a court or something to stage that kind of an intervention? Here I go again with my calamitous thoughts, but it's hard to trust what Gary is saying when he's admitted to lying about so many things already. I can't accept what he's telling me at face value. I need to make sure Beth is safe.

"For what it's worth, I think she made the right decision," Warren pipes up. "Although I'm sure you'll miss her."

Gary's lips twist into a smirk. "At least I'm free from babysitting my wife for a while."

If that's his attempt to lighten the mood, it has the opposite effect on me. What he dubs babysitting, I call control. And I know Beth felt the same way, from the rare moments she admitted as much. A cold shiver goes down my spine as my suspicions swell.

What if Beth had finally plucked up the courage to confront Gary, and he flipped out? Could he have hurt her? Tied her up in the house somewhere? Would the police be willing to do a welfare check now, if I tell them she's missing? Officer Engelmann's mistrustful expression floats to my mind. He's not going to want to hear about any more of my hunches. This time, I need to present him with evidence.

CHAPTER 19

It's been almost three weeks since Beth departed for rehab. To my immense relief, she called me a couple of days after she left and apologized for taking off in the early hours without as much as a goodbye. I was teary-eyed on the phone when I told her I'd been on the verge of reporting her missing. I really believed Gary had done something to her. The nightmarish visions I was wrestling with at night were blurring with reality.

I've tried calling her a couple of times since, but she never picks up. I wanted to go visit her right away, but Gary told me her doctor recommended letting her settle in first. He said it would be upsetting to her new routine to have visitors too early in the program. I thought about ignoring his advice, but Warren said I should go with the general consensus — for Beth's sake, if for no other reason. I couldn't argue with that, so I didn't push it.

By now, I feel as though she's had plenty of time to settle in, so I'm going to raise the issue again and see how Gary reacts. Amber has agreed to go with me to visit Beth, as soon as Gary gives us the green light. Theoretically, I don't need his permission, but he hasn't exactly been forthcoming with details, and I have no idea where the rehab facility is located. When I asked him about it, he mumbled something about it being several hours from here, which wasn't particularly helpful.

I've invited Gary and Amber over for dinner tonight, and forewarned Warren that I intend to raise the topic of visiting Beth again. He thinks I should wait until she returns my call. But I'm tired of waiting for a phone call that might never come. Gary might have told her not to call me back, for all I know. And it's not as if she has any other friends checking up on her. I'm not overly worried about her now that I know she's in a safe place — I just want her to feel as though she has someone in her corner who cares about her. And I'm not sure Gary does. The test results on the smoothie came back negative, so at least my fears that he was drugging her were misplaced. It appears Officer Engelmann was spot on, and Beth really did relapse.

Amber arrives for dinner a half-hour early. "I made apple crumble and homemade ice cream for dessert," she announces.

"Yum! You went all out," I say. "You could have just picked something up."

"Anything to grease the wheels." She winks at me. "Gary can hardly turn down our request to visit Beth after eating my crumble — guaranteed to melt even the hardest heart."

"It's about time Beth had a visitor," I say. "I don't think Gary's been to see her once since he dropped her off. He's been going to work every day as usual and his car's always there on the weekends."

"What a loser!" Amber exclaims. "I can't imagine my Jeff or your Warren abandoning us in a rehab facility for weeks on end, without even bothering to come see us."

I grimace as I stab a fork into the baked potatoes. "To be honest, I think Gary's enjoying his freedom. He was pretty up front about looking forward to getting a break from 'babysitting' her."

"Controlling her, more like it," Amber retorts. "Keeping tabs on everything she ate and did, not to mention denying her basic freedoms like driving herself around and having lunch with her neighbors."

I stiffen at the sound of the doorbell. "There he is," I say, wiping my hands on my apron.

"I'll get it!" Warren calls, jogging down the stairs fresh from the shower. "Come on in, Gary," I hear him say.

Gary seems on edge when he comes into the kitchen, his gaze skating uncertainly around the room. I pour him a glass of wine and push a plate of chips and some dips across the island to him. "How was your day?" I ask.

"Long." He reaches for a chip and trails it aimlessly through a dish of salsa, avoiding my eyes. I'm not sure if he doesn't want to be here, or if he just doesn't know what to say. Admittedly, we've had our fair share of unpleasant exchanges, which makes this dinner somewhat awkward. Thankfully, Warren offers to take him out to the garage to show him his custom-built workbench. From what I've seen, Gary's not much of a hobbyist, but it gives me a few minutes to finish up the dinner prep.

Amber helps me carry the platters of food into the dining room, then goes to the garage to call the men in for dinner. Gary takes his seat, looking, if anything, even more agitated than when he first walked in. I was hoping Warren would have managed to put him at ease by now, but, evidently, something's bothering him. He's barely touched his wine, and he doesn't appear to be hungry either — going through the motions of chewing and swallowing, but not looking like he's enjoying it. Somehow, we keep up a stream of banal conversation until dessert is served.

"So, how's Beth doing?" Amber asks, setting a plate of apple crumble and ice cream in front of Gary. "Kay and I were thinking about going to visit her one day this week."

He drops his gaze to the plate in front of him and promptly bursts into tears.

"Gary! I'm so sorry!" Amber says, sliding into the seat next to him and squeezing his shoulder. "I didn't mean to upset you. I know you must be missing Beth." She grimaces across the table at me, signaling wildly for help.

I don't know what to say either. In the face of Gary's wholly unexpected display of emotion, I feel incredibly guilty for thinking he didn't care. He's obviously more cut up about Beth being gone than I gave him credit for. I chew on my lip, wondering how best to handle the situation.

Warren clears his throat, unexpectedly bailing me out. "It's not a bad idea, Gary. Beth might enjoy a visit from the girls now that she's had a chance to settle in."

Gary wipes the back of his hand over his eyes, and sniffs back more tears. "Too late for that. She's gone for good this time."

CHAPTER 20

Amber locks a panicked gaze on me, and I see the same confusion on her face that I feel inside. *Gone for good.* I must have misheard Gary, or maybe he misspoke. Beth's not dead. He can't mean that. She's in a rehab facility — a three-month program, possibly nine. They're taking good care of her. Gary's just upset because he misses her, that's all. But she'll be back before he knows it. I knead the skin on my knuckles, trying to decide how best to clarify exactly what Gary meant, without upsetting him any further.

Warren beats me to it. "Gary, are you saying what I think you're saying?"

He gives a pathetic nod, shoulders shaking, still staring down at nothing in particular. "She's gone. Beth's dead. She passed away."

"When . . . when did this happen?" Amber asks in a half-whisper.

"Last week." Gary starts to sob again. "They were supposed to be watching her. It was their job to get her healthy. They're responsible for this!"

My spine goes rigid. It can't be true. Beth can't be gone. We just had coffee together a couple of weeks ago. I watched her devour my muffins right in front of my nose. My thoughts scatter in myriad directions. Why didn't Gary tell us sooner? How did Beth die — was she sick? Did they do an autopsy? Did he have her cremated? The thought of not even being able to lay flowers at her final resting place fills me with excruciating sadness. I care about my neighbors. Things like this aren't supposed to happen on my watch.

"How . . . how did she die?" I ask, trying to quell the churning in my stomach at the awful turn this dinner has taken. How could Gary have sat through the entire meal and only now decided to tell us that Beth is dead?

"She hung herself," he rasps.

"Oh, Gary," Amber soothes, laying a hand on his arm. "I'm so sorry. That must have been an awful shock."

He shakes her hand off and jams his fists to his eyeballs. "I don't want sympathy. I just want justice for Beth."

"I'm sure the facility's investigating her death," I say. "They'll get to the bottom of how this could have happened to a patient in their care."

Gary sniffs. "An internal investigation won't accomplish squat. They'll recommend some new procedures and call it good. I've hired a lawyer. I'm going to sue them for everything they're worth. I don't care about the money. I just want to hold them accountable for their negligence."

"I don't blame you," Warren says. "I would do the same thing if it were Kay." He gives me a bleak smile, but I can't summon a smile in return. This is too horrific to process.

"What's the name of the facility she was in?" I ask.

Gary throws me a mildly irritated look, before dissolving into tears again. "Summit, no . . . Serenity something-or-other — Wellness Clinic, Center. What does it matter?"

Warren frowns at me and gives a tiny shake of his head. He's right. This isn't the time to drill for details. Gary needs our support, not an interrogation. But alarm bells are ringing again. Why is he always so evasive?

"You should have told us right away so we could have been there for you," I say. "I can't believe you've been keeping this all to yourself for a week now."

"My lawyer told me not to talk with anyone about it. He doesn't want to risk compromising my case against the facility." Gary lets out a weighty breath. "I need you to keep this to yourselves for now. At least until the lawsuit is over and done with. As far as the other neighbors are concerned, Beth's still in rehab."

I exchange an uncertain look with Amber and Warren. I'm not thrilled about the prospect of lying to my neighbors, but I don't want to jeopardize the chance of getting justice for what happened to Beth either. "Of course," I reassure Gary. "You can tell them yourself when the time is right. But I have to ask, did Beth leave a suicide note?"

He shakes his head. "No, nothing like that."

"I just can't believe it," I say. "She never hinted that she was feeling suicidal during any of our interactions."

"It's always been an issue with her," Gary replies. "Like I told you, she's struggled with clinical depression for years." He exhales another deep breath and gets to his feet. "If you don't mind, I'd like to go home now. I'm emotionally spent, and I just want to fall into bed."

Warren escorts Gary to the door while Amber and I clean up the kitchen, a weighty silence hanging over us. When we're done, we all retire to the family room to talk it over.

"Poor Beth," Amber says. "I feel awful now that we didn't try harder to get her out of the house more often."

"We can't blame ourselves. We did our best in difficult circumstances," I say. "We didn't know she was struggling with suicidal thoughts."

"Whatever way you look at it, it's a rotten deal," Warren says, folding his hands behind his head and sinking back in an armchair. "The poor guy seems really cut up about it."

"We all are," Amber says. "It's hard to believe we went out to lunch with Beth only a few weeks back."

79

"What did Gary call that facility again?" I ask, scrolling through my phone.

"Serenity something-or-other — Wellness Clinic, I think," Warren answers.

"Weird," I say. "I don't see it listed anywhere. There's a Serenity Holistic Center or a Wellness Detox."

"That's got to be it, the detox place," Warren says. "The holistic center sounds more like a medical spa."

"Makes sense. I'll try the detox place first," I say, dialing the number.

Warren throws me an incredulous look. "What are you doing?"

"Calling them." I put a finger to my lips.

"Kay, you need to stay out of this," he implores. "They're not going to give out any information about Beth's death, especially not when they're being sued."

I arch a brow at him as I wait for someone to pick up. "You're assuming she's really dead. I'm not going to take Gary's word for it."

CHAPTER 21

I spend the next couple of days calling around all the in-patient rehab facilities in California within driving distance, introducing myself as Beth's sister from overseas and asking for details of her passing. No one has any record of a Beth Finkel. It only serves to fire me up in my quest to find out where Gary took her and what really happened to her. Warren is of the opinion that Gary misled us about the facility's name so we wouldn't interfere in the litigation process. He thinks we should stay out of it and give Gary his privacy, but the whole affair has left me unsettled. The nightmares are back, and they're worse than ever before — full-blown hallucinations where I wake up sweating, imagining Beth's corpse is sitting in a chair in the corner of the bedroom pointing an accusing finger at me.

When I meet Amber for coffee in town later that day, she's equally uneasy about the situation. "It's weird, but what can we do about it? I mean, we can't exactly report her missing, can we?"

I shrug. "Well, she is, isn't she? It's not as if I've been able to locate the rehab facility she was supposedly a patient at."

"You're assuming it was in California. What if it was farther afield — in Nevada, or Arizona, or Idaho, or Utah — who knows where?"

"It must have been in California. Gary said they left at 4.00 a.m. that morning. He was back that same evening."

Amber sips her coffee, a reflective look on her face. "They might have caught a flight. He didn't say they drove there, did he?"

I stare at her, considering the possibility for the first time. It hadn't even occurred to me that Beth might have gone out of state for treatment — that would explain why Gary never visited her. There must be hundreds of facilities within a day's flight of Los Angeles. I can't possibly call every single one of them, trying to wheedle the information out of them with my phony overseas sister story. I'll have to resort to a more underhanded tactic to get my hands on the address of the facility — namely, slipping into the rental house when Gary is at work. If Beth really was admitted to a rehab center, there must be documentation to prove it.

My phone begins to ring, and I check the screen. "It's Maria Torres. She's probably wondering if I'm home. I was admiring her garden the other day and she offered to drop off some seedlings for me." I take the call and put it on speaker. "Hey, Maria, how are you?"

"As well as old bones can be. It's a beautiful day and I've been enjoying sitting out in the garden with Smokey and Flora. How are you doing?"

"Great, thanks. I'm having coffee with Amber, and I was just telling her how beautiful your garden looks this spring."

"Thank you, dear. I'll stop by with those seedlings as soon as I get a chance. The reason I'm calling is that I got a strange note in my mailbox this morning."

"Oh?" I raise my brows at Amber. "What did it say?"

"I have to admit, it was rather upsetting. It said, *Beth Finkel's a thief.* It wasn't signed and I didn't recognize the handwriting. I was wondering if it might have been those rambunctious teenagers trying to put the blame on that poor woman now that she's in rehab."

I grimace, preparing to play along with the lie that Gary has asked us to repeat. It's still surreal to think that Beth's

82

dead. I can't bring myself to believe it — not without proof. But maybe it's just wishful thinking on my part. It strikes me as odd timing that the note showed up in Maria's mailbox just now. I can't imagine who could have written it, or why. Surely Gary wouldn't throw his dead wife under the bus like that — he was adamant Beth hadn't taken the purse to begin with. But I'm certain none of the other neighbors would have sent Maria such a disturbing note. If they knew something about the stolen purse, they would have come straight to me with the information.

"You're probably right, Maria. I think the best thing to do is just to ignore it. Maybe it was a dare of some kind, or it might have been meant as a joke — not a very funny one under the circumstances, but kids will be kids."

"Well, I don't want to make a fuss and get them in trouble, but it's always best to keep the HOA updated in case we have other incidents down the line."

I reassure her that she did the right thing and tell her not to hesitate to call again if anything else happens.

"That's kind of creepy," Amber says when I end the call. "The only person who would have known if Beth had stolen the purse is Gary. But why would he send an anonymous note exposing her as a thief now that she's dead?"

If she's dead. I fleetingly consider telling Amber about my plan to slip into Gary's house and take a look around for clues as to Beth's whereabouts for the past few weeks, but I restrain myself. The fewer people who know about my trespassing intentions, the better.

Pulling into the driveway on my return home, I notice an attractive young woman knocking on Gary's front door. An unfamiliar silver Nissan is parked at the curb. I keep my head down, pretending to be looking for something on the passenger seat, all the while keeping a close eye on the woman. I don't recognize her as a local. My thoughts dart off in myriad directions. She doesn't appear to be selling anything, but I've never known Gary or Beth to have visitors before. Surely Gary isn't seeing someone else already. The thought shoots through me like a poison arrow. It gives him a strong motive for getting rid of his wife.

After a few minutes, the woman peers over her shoulder, then crouches down and checks beneath the planter by the front door. My heart begins to race. She must be looking for a key. Is she going to try and break in? Could this be the same person who stole Maria's purse? She's well-dressed — by all appearances, she poses no threat. Most people wouldn't question her actions, but I'm not most people. I'm well aware that crooks come in all shapes and sizes, and they know how to blend into a neighborhood. I watch as she stands, and then throws another glance around her before walking briskly down the side of the house. Now I'm certain her intention is to break in — brazen of her, considering she must have heard me pull up next door. I scramble out of my car and slam the door as loudly as I can.

"Hello! Can I help you?" I call out to the woman as I hurry across the lawn to intercept her.

She scans me up and down, looking a little taken aback by my intrusive introduction. "I . . . don't think so. It doesn't look like anyone's home right now."

"Do you know the people who live here?" I ask, not willing to divulge any information before I know whom I'm talking to.

"Yes. I'm Luna Webster, Beth's daughter."

CHAPTER 22

"I just arrived back in the States from Japan yesterday," Luna says. "I hope I'm at the right address."

Beth's daughter. Not Gary's new lover, after all. I'm slightly ashamed that I immediately thought the worst of him when he's still in mourning. I stand there dumbstruck for a moment, unsure what to say or do, before my sense of hospitality kicks in. "I'm sorry, I didn't realize you were family. I'm Kay Mellows. I live next door. Why don't you come in and wait with me until Gary gets back?"

Luna glances at her watch, seeming to consider my offer. "Do you think they'll be much longer?"

I flinch at the question. There is no more *they*. But apparently, Luna doesn't know that. I assumed she'd returned from overseas after hearing about her mother's death. But, if she was estranged from her, it's possible it's just an unfortunate coincidence that she has shown up now. I'm not sure what the ethical thing to do is. Should I tell her that her mother is dead, or wait and let her stepfather break the news to her?

"I'm guessing an hour or so," I say breezily.

A relieved look flickers over Luna's face. "In that case, I'll take you up on your offer."

She follows me across the lawn, and I lead her through to the kitchen and offer her something to drink.

"Just some water would be great, thanks. I'm always so dehydrated after flying long distance."

I grab two bottles from the fridge and hand her one. "What were you doing in Japan?"

"I was teaching English. I just finished up a three-year contract." She fiddles with the lid on her water bottle. "I needed to get away for a bit after Mom and Gary got hitched. I was mad at her for marrying him. Gary was a friend of Dad's. It felt like a betrayal of sorts, even though Dad had passed away two years earlier. We were very close, my dad and I."

I meld my features into a portrait of compassion. I'm truly moved by her story, but I'm also eager to learn everything I can about the Finkels' relationship. Clearly, they didn't meet at a grief group like Beth led me to believe. "I'm so sorry for your loss."

Luna flutters her long, thick lashes as though fighting back tears. "Dad contracted pancreatic cancer. It was stage four when they discovered it. There was nothing they could do for him."

I nod along as the words spill from her lips. Beth said she lost her daughter at nineteen — was that the last time she saw her, perhaps? Luna doesn't look to be a day past twenty-five, if that. She's a beautiful girl, although I can't see much, if any, resemblance to Beth. I'm guessing she takes after the father she clearly idolized. I can't imagine how she's going to react when she learns that her mother is gone now too. For once, I'm eager to hear the sound of Gary's BMW pulling into the driveway. The longer I spend talking with Luna, the more I feel like a hypocrite for hiding the truth from her.

I ask about her years in Japan — more to pass the time until Gary gets home than anything else — and she happily regales me with some of her culinary and cultural adventures. Gary's usually home by five thirty but when six o'clock rolls around and there's still no sign of him, I feel like I've pushed it as far as I can. I should probably break the news to Luna.

Warren will be home shortly from his business dinner, and I'd rather get it over with before he walks in.

"Luna," I say gently, setting down my water, "there's something I need to tell you. I was hoping your stepdad would have been home by now so he could tell you himself, but it looks like he might be working late tonight. It's not fair to keep you in the dark any longer. I'm really sorry, honey, but your mom passed away a week ago."

Her mouth drops open, conflicting emotions flitting across her face in quick succession — disbelief, shock, denial, grief. Her bottom lip begins to quiver. "How? I mean, was it an accident? What happened? Gary drives too fast — Mom always says that." Tears begin sliding down her face. "He hit a deer one time and almost killed them both. Mom was begging him to slow down because it was dark and foggy and they were lost. But he wouldn't listen. He's so . . ." She breaks off mid-sentence and throws me a helpless look. "Is he dead too?"

"No. Gary's fine." I twist my hands in my lap. "I'm truly sorry. I didn't know your mom very long, but she seemed like a sweet lady."

Luna tucks a strand of hair behind her ear and wipes her eyes. "She had her struggles, but she was still my mother. I shouldn't have been so self-righteous about her decision to marry Gary. I only took the job overseas in the first place to punish her. I wish I'd never left her alone with him. I knew he couldn't be trusted to take care of her."

I do my best to mask my surprise. Even back then, Luna must have picked up on something about Gary that didn't sit right with her. Maybe she'll be receptive to my suspicions, but I need to tread carefully and remind myself that she's grief-stricken and vulnerable. "You can't blame yourself for what happened. For what it's worth, Gary seemed to take it very hard."

"I doubt that. The man has no feelings." Luna rumples her brow, a hint of suspicion in her eyes. "You haven't told me yet how Mom died."

My stomach knots with dread. "I . . . don't have all the details, Luna. I only know what Gary told me, although I'm not sure I believe him entirely. He said she was in rehab — an in-patient program." I hesitate and clear my throat. "She took her own life while she was there."

Luna covers her mouth with her hand. "You mean she OD'd?"

I press my lips tightly together. "I don't believe so, but, like I said, I don't have all the specifics."

"That doesn't make any sense," Luna cries, the desperation in her eyes gnawing at me. "Why would she check in to rehab in the first place? She doesn't take drugs. She's not an addict. She doesn't even drink anymore."

I frown, wondering if I should mention the vodka bottle I saw sitting on the counter and the haggard state I found Beth in on multiple occasions. But it's speculation on my part. I haven't ruled out the possibility that Gary staged it for my benefit.

"I don't know why your mom went to rehab," I admit. "I was just as surprised as you are when I found out. You'll have to talk to Gary about it when he gets home. I haven't been able to get much information out of him."

Luna's eyes widen in momentary panic. She reaches for her purse. "I should go wait in my car. It's probably best if he doesn't know I talked to you. Do you know which rehab facility my mom was in? I'd like to speak with the director."

I rub the back of my neck, wondering how honest I should be with her. Should I tell her I think Gary's hiding something? That I can't find any trace of the facility Beth was supposedly admitted to? That I don't think she killed herself?

Or maybe I should just come right out with it and tell Luna what I'm most afraid of — that Gary did something to her mother.

CHAPTER 23

"Do you have an address for the place?" Luna asks.

She's looking at me again with those pleading eyes. My heart breaks for her. Maybe it's because I don't have a daughter of my own, but my instincts are to take her in my arms and hug her, to make her hot chocolate with whipped cream, and even offer to let her stay the night — or as long as she wants, for that matter. She must be reeling from shock now that she's lost the chance to repair the relationship with her mom. By the sound of it, she didn't have much of one with Gary to begin with.

The more I think about it, I don't think she'd be safe staying next door. If Gary did kill Beth, what's to stop him from killing Luna too if she challenges his story? He must know how she feels about her dad's best friend marrying her mother. And now that Beth's gone, emotions will be riding high on both sides. It's too dangerous for her to stay in the house alone with him. I wasn't able to protect Beth, but I can try to do something to protect her daughter. First, I need to convince her that she's in danger. I have to come clean about my suspicion that everything Gary told me was a lie. Much as I want to shield her from the horror of it, she's an adult — she can handle the truth.

"Luna," I say, sliding forward in my seat, "in all honesty, I'm not sure your mother ever went to a rehab facility. She never hinted to me in any of the conversations I had with her that she was planning on it. Gary told me they left that morning at 4.00 a.m. to go to the facility, but I've never been able to get any more information about it out of him. When I pressed him for details, he gave me a couple of versions of the name, but I haven't been able to locate the place. I don't know if it's in state, or out of state, or if it even exists. No one saw your mother leave the house that morning." I bite my lip before forcing myself to continue. "I can't even be sure she was alive when they left."

The color drains from Luna's face, her voice dropping to a whisper. "Are you saying you think Gary might have killed her?"

I raise my palms, an apologetic grimace on my face. "I know it sounds outrageous. But something's not adding up. Gary had essentially cut Beth off from the outside world. He was very controlling, but she wasn't in a position to fight back — she wasn't thinking straight. She was weak and confused. He dictated everything she was allowed to eat, and when. He made smoothies for her every morning and stood over her to make sure she drank them. I'm convinced he was drugging her before he left for work. I managed to sneak a sample out of the house and had it tested. It came back negative, but I have a feeling he deliberately left that tumbler with the dregs of an undoctored smoothie for me to find. He knew I was growing suspicious and that I was checking up on Beth while he was at work."

Luna pulls at the sleeve of her shirt. "There must be some way to verify his story about the rehab facility. He can't legally keep information about my mom's death from me." A lone tear trickles down her cheek, sending my motherly instincts into overdrive. She may be an adult, but at the moment, she looks like a lost chick chirping in vain for a mother who will never return to the nest. I have to do what I can to help her.

"I'm not sure of the legalities of disclosing health information," I say. "We'll have to ask a lawyer about that. We could try and locate a death certificate, but that typically takes a few weeks before it's publicly available. The other problem is, I'm not sure which state Beth was in when she supposedly died."

"I can't wait that long," Luna says. "I have to know what happened to my mother and where she was when she passed. I have every right to know. I can't deny I'm not a little afraid of Gary, but I need to get the information from him somehow. I don't even know where my mother's remains are."

"I understand, but I don't think it's a good idea for you to stay with him under the circumstances," I say.

Luna throws out her hands in a despairing gesture. "I literally just got back from Japan. I have nowhere else to live."

"You're welcome to stay here with me and my husband as long as you need to." The words spill out before I have time to consider them. Warren will berate me later for not consulting with him first, but it's not up for negotiation. It's the decent thing to do. I didn't do enough to save her mother, and Luna is all alone in the world now.

She pulls out a tissue and blows her nose. "That's very kind of you, Kay, but I think I'll have a better chance of finding out what happened if I stay with my stepdad, at least for tonight. It would look weird if I opted to stay with a stranger instead."

I give a reluctant nod. "In that case, let me have your phone number so I can text you and make sure you're okay."

We exchange numbers, and I make her promise to text me the following morning — sooner if she feels in the least bit unsafe. I can get to the loaded gun in our safe a whole lot quicker than the police can get here.

At the sound of an engine, I jump up and run to the window. "That's Gary pulling into the driveway now."

Luna frantically wipes at her wet cheeks. "I need him to think I don't know that my mother's dead yet. Let's see if the story he tells me jives with what he told you."

CHAPTER 24

I let Luna out the back door so she can slip around the side of the house and wait until Gary goes inside before knocking on his door. I hope I'm doing the right thing by letting her stay with him, not that I have much choice in the matter. I watch from behind the curtains in the family room as Luna makes her way up to the front door of the rental and disappears inside. The minute she does, I call Amber and update her on this unexpected new development, promising to keep her apprised of the situation.

I'm flicking restlessly through channels on the television when Warren arrives home a little after 8.30 p.m.

"How was your dinner?" I ask, nibbling on my fingernail.

"It went well; we got the contract. It's a big one." He slips off his coat and hangs it on the rack in the hallway. He goes in for a hug, then hesitates, cocking his head to one side. "What's wrong?"

I wasn't planning on unloading on him the minute he walked through the door, but he knows me too well. I grab him by the hand and pull him down next to me on the couch. "You're never going to believe what happened. Beth's daughter, Luna, showed up a little while ago."

His brows shoot up. "You're kidding me! I thought they were estranged. How did she find out her mother had passed away?"

"That's the sad part about it. She didn't have a clue. I had to break the news to her. She just got back from a three-year stint teaching English in Japan, and I think she was hoping to mend some bridges with her mother. She certainly didn't come here for Gary's sake."

Warren scrubs a hand over his jaw, a pained look on his face. "Poor girl. She must be devastated." He jerks his chin in the direction of the house next door. "Is she over there right now?"

I nod. "Yes, unfortunately. I offered to let her stay here, but she doesn't think it would go over well with Gary. She's probably right. She wants to try and get as much information as possible from him about what happened to Beth when she supposedly took her own life."

"Supposedly?" Warren echoes, picking up on my skeptical tone.

"Well, we only have Gary's word for it, don't we?"

"You're doing it again, Kay — you need to back off. I hope you didn't fill Luna's head with your conspiracy theories." Warren sighs. "I need a drink. Want one?"

"Sure," I say, following him into the kitchen. I haven't finished making my case yet for why we need to take an active interest in Luna's safety. I can tell Warren's not sold on the idea of meddling in their affairs. He pours us each a glass of pinot grigio and sits down at the table.

"I'm not dabbling in conspiracy theories," I say, fiddling with the stem of my glass. "There's no evidence whatsoever that Beth went to rehab."

"What are you suggesting?" he asks, eyeing me curiously.

I spend the next few minutes going over everything I told Luna, then wait with bated breath for Warren's reaction. Unlike me, he never says the first thing that comes to mind. He needs time to process his thoughts. I've always appreciated that about him, even though it drives me nuts at the same time. I can count on him to think things through in a rational manner and pull me back from the edge when I catapult into reactive chaos. For once, I'm certain he'll be forced to agree with my hunch that Gary is lying about what really happened to Beth. Everything I've learned since our first unsettling interaction with our renters has only confirmed my suspicion that Gary Finkel is a duplicitous and dangerous man.

"Those are some pretty serious allegations you're making," Warren says, reaching for his glass.

"Yes, but if they're true, Beth's daughter could be in danger. And it's our obligation to help her. We rented our house to a maniac, and she's over there with him, all alone."

Warren sips his wine, unruffled as ever. "I don't think she's in any immediate danger. Gary would have a hard time explaining the disappearance of his stepdaughter right after his wife's death. If your hunch is right, then he won't make any rash moves. He spent weeks painting a picture of Beth as an addict and making sure everyone's perception of her was tainted. And it worked. No one questioned him when he told them she'd gone to a rehab facility."

"Except me," I retort.

Warren tips his head in acknowledgment. "Except for you. But then you question everything."

I throw him a piqued look. "You can't take what people tell you at face value. I don't know exactly what's going on next door, but Gary is definitely hiding something."

Warren nods thoughtfully. "Maybe it's not what you think. Maybe Beth finally left him, and he's too ashamed to admit it."

"That would be the best-case scenario," I say, getting to my feet and pacing across the floor. "Whatever way this shakes out, I'm not going to stop digging until I get to the bottom of what's really going on. Unless I see Beth's death certificate with my own eyes, I won't believe she's really dead."

CHAPTER 25

I woke up around midnight sweating and screaming, and it took Warren a good half-hour to calm me down. Neither of us slept properly after that, jerking in and out of fitful bouts of sleep. I felt guilty when I saw the mottled shadows beneath his eyes this morning, but he didn't complain or badger me about the amount of stress I'm putting us both under.

I've sent Luna several texts over the past couple of hours, but she hasn't texted me back. Her car hasn't moved from the street, so I know she didn't leave the house — at least, not of her own accord. *Stop it, Kay!* I can't go there. I need to pull myself together and not ruminate on illogical thoughts and half-baked theories. I reach for a notepad and begin making a list of mindless chores to distract myself with.

Despite my valiant efforts, I'm beside myself with worry, so, after a few more minutes, I cave and call Amber to vent. "I'm worried something's happened to Luna. She promised she would text me this morning. I've sent her several messages, but she hasn't responded to any of them. I can't focus on work until I know for sure she's okay. Do you think I should go next door and check on her? Gary already left, so the coast's clear."

"Breathe! It's only nine thirty," Amber replies. "If she's jet-lagged, she might be sleeping in. Let her rest."

"I suppose you're right," I say, trying to convince myself. "It's not as if Gary took off in the middle of the night. I saw his car pull out around seven thirty this morning. I'll give it a little longer."

I hang up after promising to let Amber know the minute I hear from Luna. I take my coffee over to my desk and settle into work. The morning slips by and, before I know it, it's noon. I do a quick calculation of the time difference between Japan and California. It's hard to imagine Luna could still be sleeping off her jet lag. I can't help wondering if Gary is up to his old tricks and drugged her before he left for work. I can't bear the uncertainty any longer.

Abandoning my computer, I hurry next door and stab frantically at the doorbell. After repeated attempts, I walk around to the back of the house and jiggle the doorknob to no avail. I peer through the kitchen window but there's no sign of Luna anywhere. I'm tempted to use my front door key to go inside the house, but Gary would call the cops on me, and if Luna turns out to be sleeping peacefully in bed, I won't have a leg to stand on. No probable cause — just an overzealous neighbor, as Officer Engelmann has already concluded I am.

I'm walking back around to the front of the house when I spot Gary's BMW turning onto the street. My chest constricts. What is he doing home so early? Has he made plans with Luna? I sprint across the lawn to my own yard and start winding up the hose as though I've just finished watering my flowers.

"You're home early," I say, when he climbs out of his car.

"Yeah," he grunts.

When he doesn't elaborate, I gesture to the Nissan. "Any idea whose car that is?"

He hesitates before answering. "Oh, yeah, that's my stepdaughter's."

I straighten up, giving him my full attention. "Your step-daughter's? When did she get here?"

"Last night. Late."

I arrange my face into an expression of concern. "How did she take the news about her mother?"

He shrugs. "She wasn't too bothered. They hadn't spoken in years — her choice. She only came by to pick up some stuff she'd left with us."

I'm momentarily stunned into silence. I know from Luna's reaction yesterday that he's most definitely lying. My heartbeat picks up pace. I can't shake the feeling that Luna might be in danger. "Warren and I would love to meet her," I say. "Why don't you two come over for dinner tonight?"

Gary glances away, scratching his forehead. He's stalling — trying to come up with some plausible excuse as to why they can't make it. My pulse thunders in my ears. I'm almost certain now that Luna's in trouble. I try to keep my expression impassive when all I want to do is rush past him and break down the door.

"Luna went to visit Beth's sister in Portland," he says at length. "She caught an early flight this morning."

"What?" I gasp, before I can catch myself. "But . . . her car's still here." I can't believe Luna would leave without letting me know, not after everything I told her. "Why would she take off already when she only just got here?" I ask.

Gary narrows his eyes at me. "Why are you so interested in what she does? It's hardly any of your business."

I shrug and hang the hose back on the reel. "No reason, other than that I'd like to meet Beth's daughter and offer her my condolences."

"I'll be sure to pass them along," Gary says, before turning his back on me and striding up to the front door. Without another glance in my direction, he disappears inside, slamming the door behind him.

I stand in my yard for a long moment, shaking inside, wondering what exactly he's hiding behind that door. Is he holding Luna prisoner? I need to do something. I can't let him get away with this — not when two women have gone missing right under my nose.

I hurry into the house and pick up the phone. The last person Officer Engelmann wants to hear from is me, but today's not his lucky day.

CHAPTER 26

Officer Engelmann doesn't answer his phone, so I'm forced to leave a message. I keep it brief and generic, knowing he'll likely ignore anything that hints of histrionics. To my chagrin, he doesn't return my call until the following morning, and he doesn't sound particularly thrilled to be doing so.

"Mrs. Mellows — Kay," he begins, with a loud exhale. "What can I do for you *today*?"

Clearly, I need to get straight to the point.

"I'm calling about my next-door neighbor's stepdaughter."

"Uh-huh. Are we talking about the same neighbor you suspected of drugging his wife?"

I ignore the undertone of sarcasm and plow on. "Yes, that's right. Gary Finkel. His wife, Beth, passed away last week."

I leave him hanging for a moment or two to let that sink in. "According to Gary, she took her own life in a rehab facility."

"I'm very sorry to hear that," Officer Engelmann replies in an annoyingly noncommittal tone. "How can I help you?"

"Gary's stepdaughter, Luna, showed up at the house the day before yesterday. She had no idea that her mother was deceased. She recently returned to the States after working overseas for several years. She stayed at Gary's place the night

99

before last, and now she's disappeared. I've tried texting her multiple times, but I haven't heard from her, and I still can't get ahold of her. I questioned Gary about it yesterday when he got home from work, and he told me she'd caught an early morning flight to visit her aunt in Portland." I gulp a quick breath and continue, almost tripping over my words in my haste to get to the punchline. "I know from talking with Luna that she had no plans to leave. I'm afraid something might have happened to her. First her mother disappeared, now Luna's followed suit. And the only common denominator is Gary Finkel. I think he—"

"Wait a minute, slow down," Engelmann interrupts. "I thought you said Luna's mother passed away."

"So Gary claims, but he hasn't exactly been forthcoming with any details. When I asked him for the name of the rehab facility Beth was in, he brushed me off with a couple of vague variations of the name. I've been calling around, but I still haven't been able to find the place. I'm really worried that Gary might have had something to do with her disappearance too. It's suspicious to me that both Beth and Luna vanished without a trace, and I'm stuck relying on Gary's explanations as to where they're at. As their landlord, I feel responsible for their safety."

"To be clear, your renter's not under any obligation to disclose personal information regarding his wife's medical history," Engelmann replies. "And it's not unreasonable to think that Beth's daughter might have gone to visit her aunt at a time like this."

"But Gary can't be trusted. He's lied to me about other things before," I snap.

Engelmann coughs politely. "I appreciate your concern for your neighbors' welfare, but—"

"Can't you at least look into it — do a welfare check or something?" I cry. "Two women have gone missing from my rental. I think that's newsworthy, don't you? Maybe I should post the story on social media and enlist some volunteers to help me find them, if the cops can't do anything."

Engelmann is silent for a moment, as though mulling over my words.

"It's not just an empty threat," I add. "I'll involve the media, if that's what it takes to get someone to look into this."

"All right." He gives a long-suffering sigh. "Leave it with me. I'll make a call to Mr. Finkel and try to ease your mind about the situation, under the condition you don't blow this up into a spectacle."

"Thank you," I say, exhaling in relief. "I appreciate you taking this seriously. Trust me, something stinks about the whole situation. There were red flags the first time I met Gary Finkel, and it's only gotten worse since."

"I can't promise to get back to you today," Engelmann says. "But I'll do my best to get ahold of the guy."

I give him Gary's mobile number, only too aware that he'll know for sure it was me who called for a welfare check. But it doesn't deter me. I hang up, relieved that the police are actually going to do something, and worried about how long it's going to take them to get around to it. My hunch is that Luna is still in the house. She could be tied up inside one of the bedrooms, drugged, or possibly even dead — like her mother. My skin crawls at the disturbing thought of two bodies rotting inside those walls. I'm beginning to think the only rehab Beth encountered was at Gary's hands.

I set my laptop up on a TV table in the family room so I can keep an eye out the window for any sign of people coming or going next door. At lunchtime, I munch on a sandwich in front of my laptop, only leaving my vantage spot for a couple of much-needed bathroom breaks.

By mid-afternoon, I can stand it no longer. I still haven't heard back from Officer Engelmann, and I'm worried that Luna's chances of getting out of the house alive will diminish once Gary returns from work. I need to take action now. I shoot Amber a quick text.

Luna's missing. Using my key to enter the rental. If you don't hear from me in the next thirty minutes, call the police.

I consider bringing my gun, but I'll hardly need it — I just have to get in and out before Gary returns home. I retrieve a spare key from the rack in the mudroom, exit through the back door, and slip through the adjoining gate between the yards. I take a couple of minutes to survey the area around the door, checking for cameras. I wouldn't put it past Gary to have installed an extra one at the back of the house strictly for my benefit. My phone chimes with a reply from Amber.

Are you crazy? Do NOT do this!

I don't bother responding. Maybe I am crazy, but it's a calculated risk. Surely the cops can't arrest me for trespassing when I own the house, although I could be mistaken. I'm unfamiliar with renters' rights and privacy laws. This is the first time Warren and I have managed a rental, so we're learning as we go.

Before I can talk myself out of it, I make a beeline for the door and unlock it. Slipping inside, I close the door and press my back to it, scarcely daring to breathe. I'm half afraid Gary might be hiding inside, waiting on me to do something so utterly predictable. I feel like he can read my mind at times.

Once my thumping heart rate starts to slow to a more normal speed, I take a look around the kitchen. It barely looks lived in — no dirty dishes in the sink, no mail on the counter, no fruit in the ceramic bowl I agonized over at TJ Maxx. It almost feels as though the house has been abandoned. In a way it has, with Beth gone, and now Luna too.

I head out into the hallway and glance into the family room as I pass by. I don't know what I'm expecting to see — Luna relaxing in a chair, grinning at me? *So sorry I forgot to text you back. What are you up to? Breaking and entering — a bit drastic, don't you think?*

Slowly, I make my way up the stairs, listening for any sound that would indicate the presence of someone else in the house, all the while throwing regular glances over my shoulder. I keep getting the creepy feeling that Gary is following me. I've watched too many scary movies where the bad guy is right behind their hapless victim, matching their every foot-step until they're ready to pounce.

Upstairs, the doors to the bedrooms are closed. I enter the primary first, and quickly check the en-suite bathroom and closet, but there's no sign of anyone. I move on down the hall to the second bedroom that overlooks the backyard. I reach for the door handle, but it doesn't budge. "Luna," I call out. "Are you in there?"

I freeze when I notice the new lock.

CHAPTER 27

The hair on the back of my neck tingles. *I knew Gary was hiding something!* He must have locked Luna inside her room. She must have challenged his story about what happened to her mother — maybe she even found some evidence in the house to prove that Gary did something to her, and now he can't let Luna go. I've got to get her out of there.

"Hello?" I cry out, slapping my palms on the door. "Luna, are you in there? Say something, please!" I bang my fists repeatedly on the door, then press my ear to it, hoping to hear some kind of a sound, or a muted moan, anything that would justify me fetching a sledgehammer and breaking down the door. I would do it in a heartbeat if I knew for sure she was in there. But what if I'm wrong? Maybe I should opt for a less drastic approach like taking the door off its hinges. Is a landlord legally allowed to do that? If only there was a way to know for sure that Luna is in there — that would vindicate any and all measures to free her.

I bang on the door again, half screaming her name. Still no answer, but I'm not convinced she isn't in there. She could be drugged up and totally unaware that help is at hand. I can't in good conscience walk away from this locked door. It's a sure sign that something's not right. Who puts a deadbolt on the outside of a bedroom door? Gary certainly didn't get our permission to install it, which can only mean that something nefarious is going on inside. I wonder if he kept Beth locked up in there at times too.

My phone rings, and I almost jump out of my skin. I totally forgot to put it on silent. I fish it out of my pocket, and Officer Engelmann's name appears on the screen. A chill ripples across my shoulders. It's almost as though he knows what I'm up to.

"Hello?" I say, trying to hold my voice steady.

"I finally managed to get a hold of Gary Finkel," he begins. "Apparently, he's been in meetings all day. He confirmed that his stepdaughter showed up on his doorstep the night before last. He says she picked up some items that her aunt wanted and caught a flight to Portland early yesterday. He even gave me the aunt's number to call."

"But . . . Luna's car's still here."

"Maybe she took an Uber to the airport," Engelmann says, an impatient edge creeping into his tone.

"Did you call her aunt and confirm Gary's story?" I ask.

"Yes. It checked out. She's a very pleasant woman. She even passed the phone to her niece so I could have a word with her."

I stare at the shiny, new lock on the door in front of me. I can hardly believe what I'm hearing. How can Luna be in Portland when I'm in the process of trying to rescue her from this room? "You . . . spoke to Luna?"

Engelmann clears his throat. "As a matter of fact, I had quite an interesting conversation with her. She says you accosted her on her stepdad's doorstep — demanded to know what she was doing and who she was, and insisted she wait at your house for Gary to return. She says you made her feel like a criminal." He hesitates before continuing. "She also said you tried to convince her of all sorts of conspiracy theories about what Gary might have done to her mother — even forced her to give you her phone number. She found it all very distressing."

I'm speechless with shock. There are some half-truths in what he's telling me. He must have actually spoken to Luna. No one else was privy to the conversation between us. Granted, she put a spin on it that's entirely inaccurate, but the substance of it was there. A flurry of calamitous thoughts competes in my brain. I try twisting the door handle in front of me again. Am I losing it? Have I misinterpreted everything? Did Luna really fly to Portland after all? Maybe Gary has his valuables locked up in here. Or maybe it's a shrine to Beth — he could have moved all her stuff into one room, finding it too painful to look at anymore.

"Kay, are you still there?" Officer Engelmann asks.

I scrunch my eyes shut, trying to clear my thoughts. "Yes, sorry about that. Got distracted there for a minute."

"I hope that gives you some peace of mind," Engelmann continues. "Gary mentioned that he's on his way home and he'd be happy to answer any other questions you might have."

My heart leaps in my chest, the phone almost slipping from my grasp. I need to get out of this house. Gary only works thirty minutes away, on the other side of town. "Great," I mumble. "Thanks for clearing things up for me."

I ram my phone into my pocket and dart back down the stairs. I'm sure Officer Engelmann was surprised that I didn't give him any real pushback or grill him for more information, but then again, he has no idea that I'm inside Gary's house, debating whether or not to break down a door.

My fingers tremble as I lock the back door behind me, hoping against hope that my neighbor doesn't come screeching into the driveway and catch me in the act. As I dash over to the gate that separates the two backyards, I turn and look back over my shoulder.

My blood runs cold when a curtain twitches in the window of the locked upstairs bedroom.

CHAPTER 28

Back in the safety of my own house, I collapse in a heap on the couch and wait for the adrenaline pumping through my veins to subside. My mind is somersaulting all over the place, trying to rationalize my turbulent thoughts. I *did* see that curtain move, didn't I? Or was I hallucinating again? If Luna really is in Portland, who is in that bedroom? Could it possibly be Beth — alive, but locked out of sight? She was already a prisoner in her own home, figuratively speaking — so drugged up that she didn't have the presence of mind to leave. But now she might be a literal prisoner, at the mercy of a sadistic monster. Gary has told everyone she's in rehab — or dead — so no one's going to be looking for her.

But why didn't she answer when I banged on the door? Is she too out of it to realize where she is? She could be trapped in that bedroom for as long as Gary continues to rent the house from us, and no one would ever know it. She could starve to death in there. It's too horrific to fathom.

I'm so agitated I can't sit still. I chomp on my nails and pace across the room, anxiously waiting for Gary to return. I don't dare confront him about the locked room on my own. But if I call Officer Engelmann, how on earth am I going to explain to him how I know about the newly installed lock without admitting that I went inside my neighbor's house? After everything that's gone down, Engelmann's not going to want to entertain any new suspicions on my part without some hefty proof. If anything, he's going to side with Gary, especially if I accuse him of keeping his "deceased" wife a prisoner in the guest bedroom. It sounds ludicrous even to my own ears, like I'm the crazy conspiracy neighbor lady. Even Warren thinks I'm a bit much at times, with my binoculars and everything. But someone has to be the eyes and ears of the neighborhood.

It stings to know that Luna lied about me to the cops. I really thought we had bonded over Beth. I'm desperate to vent about the betrayal with Warren, but I can't tell him I was trespassing next door. Law-abiding citizen that he is, he'll freak out. Besides, I already know what he'll say if I suggest that Gary might be keeping Beth prisoner.

That's crazy thinking, Kay. You need to stop entertaining the idea that we're living next door to a serial killer. That's why you keep having these nightmares. You fantasize way too much.

It's true that my nightmares have been getting worse the longer the drama next door goes on. Often, they're so vivid that I have trouble going back to sleep afterward. The ongoing sleep deprivation is affecting my judgment, but I'm certain I didn't imagine that locked bedroom door. Although I'm beginning to wonder if that upstairs curtain really twitched at all. It could have been wishful thinking on my part. I was in a complete panic at the time, hair flying in wild abandon and partly obscuring my vision as I fled the house. I'll concede I might have been mistaken about the curtain, but not about the lock on the door.

I hit the speed dial for Amber's number and press the phone to my ear.

"Are you safe?" she blurts out, the minute the call connects.

"Yes. I'm home. Gary's on his way back."

"How do you know he's—"

"Never mind that. You're never going to believe what I found."

Amber draws in a sharp breath. "Ugh, I'm not sure I want to know. Please tell me it wasn't a body."

"I didn't get that far. Gary's installed a lock on the guest bedroom overlooking the backyard."

"That's weird, and kind of creepy. I take it he didn't ask permission?"

"No — which tells me there's something he doesn't want us to know about in there."

"Like what?" Amber's voice lowers. "You're scaring me now."

"I know it sounds crazy, but I think Gary might be keeping Beth locked up in that bedroom."

"What?" Amber makes a horrified gurgling sound. "But . . . she's dead. Are you telling me he's got her body in there?"

"No, I would have noticed a smell. The thing is, she might not be dead at all. Gary could have drugged her and locked her up in there. I hammered on the door and yelled, but no one answered."

"I don't know, Kay. It sounds like a bit of a stretch. I thought you went over there to look for Luna. What makes you think Gary isn't holding her hostage?"

"That's what I was afraid of initially, but it turns out she's in Portland, Oregon, visiting Beth's sister. I didn't believe Gary when he told me that, so I called Officer Engelmann and asked him to do a welfare check. He spoke with Luna and her aunt. I think Luna was trying to distance herself from the situation, or maybe Gary threatened her with something, because she lied about me to Engelmann. She told him I tried to convince her that Gary had done something to her mother. She said I made her feel very uncomfortable, when all I did was show her some hospitality. At any rate, Luna's not locked up next door. But someone's in that room — I know it."

Amber sighs. "Just because you have a hunch doesn't—"

"It's not just a hunch. When I was going through the gate into my yard I looked back at the window, and I saw the curtain twitch. Someone was in there, Amber."

"Are you sure about that? You've been kind of jumpy lately, not getting much sleep. Could you have imagined it? I mean, if Beth was really in there, she would have answered you when you were banging on the door."

"Not if he's holding something over her head — like her daughter."

110

CHAPTER 29

I've just hung up the phone with Amber when Gary's BMW pulls into the driveway. I watch as he walks around to the back of the car and opens the trunk. Heart thumping, I snatch up my binoculars from the coffee table and peer through them, hoping to identify what he's pulling out. It looks like his brief-case and a partially filled black trash bag. Fear coils around my heart. Could it be supplies to finish Beth off with — duct tape and rope, chemicals to dissolve her body? My thoughts spin in erratic flight patterns inside my head as every gruesome crime show scenario springs to mind. But this isn't television. Things like that don't happen in my neighborhood. At least they didn't until the Finkels moved in next door.

I try to tell myself that Gary is simply returning home from another day at work, and that there's nothing suspicious about what he's doing. After all, I don't have a shred of evidence to support the idea that he's a killer. By all appearances, his wife was an addict who sadly passed away at a rehab facility by her own hand. So what if Gary put a lock on one of the upstairs bedrooms? Lots of people have expensive computer equipment and gaming setups these days. Maybe he was afraid it might get ripped off after the break-in at Maria's place. We

111

can deduct the cost of removing the lock from his deposit when he moves out.

I doggedly turn these thoughts over in my mind, but they ring increasingly hollow. I keep seeing images of Gary squeezing Beth's elbow, finishing her sentences for her, monitoring her food, sneering about babysitting her, painting a picture of an addict with low self-esteem who needed him to function. I can't abandon her to that psycho. I have to be sure she's not locked up in that room.

By the time Warren gets home, I've worked out what we need to do. He won't like my proposition, but I'm not going to give him the option to refuse. As far as I'm concerned, it's our civic duty to make sure our renter isn't a serial killer. While Warren browses the news on his iPad, I whip up a pesto chicken pasta dish for dinner and pour him a glass of wine, hoping it will make things go more smoothly when I float my plan. I wait patiently for him to swallow a few bites before setting down my fork. "Luna's gone," I announce. "Vanished into thin air, just like Beth."

Warren stops chewing. "What do you mean? I thought she was staying with Gary. Her car's still parked on the street."

"I know. He claims she took a flight to Portland yesterday to visit Beth's sister."

Warren shrugs. "Maybe she did."

"I talked to Luna at length, and she never mentioned a trip."

Warren eyes me uneasily as he reaches for his wine glass. "What are you getting at, Kay?"

I lean back in my seat, painting an earnest expression on my face. I can't tell him about my conversation with Officer Engelmann, which confirms Gary's side of the story. Warren has to believe what I'm telling him because I need his help. "What if Gary's holding Luna against her will inside the house?" I say.

Warren groans. "Please don't start with the conspiracy theories again."

"It's not a conspiracy theory. Luna was supposed to text me, and she never did. I made her promise she would let me know she was safe. There's only one good reason why I didn't hear from her; she must be incapacitated — drugged, maybe."

Warren chases a piece of chicken around in the sauce on his plate before stabbing it and putting it in his mouth. He chews methodically for a long moment before swallowing. "Luna's grieving for her mother. She's in shock. She probably forgot to text you before she left to visit her aunt."

I take a deep breath. "I have reason to believe otherwise. You're not going to like this, Warren, but I used the spare key to get into the rental while Gary was at work."

"What? Are you out of your mind?" Beads of sweat break out on Warren's forehead. "You do know that's illegal, don't you?"

I flap a hand dismissively in his direction. "So's kidnapping."

He opens his mouth to say something, but I cut him off.

"Gary put a new deadbolt on the guest bedroom that overlooks the backyard. I couldn't get in. Why on earth would he do that unless he wanted to keep someone locked up inside?"

Warren tosses his fork on his plate. "I don't know. Maybe he has something valuable in there." He frowns across at me. "Did you hear anyone in the room?"

"No. I hammered on the door, but no one responded. I thought maybe he had sedated Luna, but then when I was crossing the lawn into our yard, I saw the curtain at that window twitch, like someone was peering around it."

Warren looks disconcerted. "You've been seeing a lot of things lately."

I jut out my chin. "I don't think it was my imagination, but I need to make sure."

"How? You can't very well call the police again with your latest speculative slant on our renter. They're going to think we're disgruntled landlords trying to find an excuse to evict Gary."

"I know the cops won't listen to me. That's why I need your help." I pause and take a quick breath before hitting him up with my proposal. "I want you to take the bedroom door off its hinges tomorrow while Gary's at work."

CHAPTER 30

It takes about an hour of arguing back and forth with Warren before I break him down and get him to agree to my "utterly reckless" plan, as he calls it. He only relented in the end because I told him I would take the door off its hinges myself if he refused to help me. He doesn't want me trashing his tools or damaging the door, which would be a dead giveaway that we'd been trespassing. Thankfully, Warren is highly skilled when it comes to handyman tasks. Gary won't even know we've been in there, unless of course, we find something nefarious behind the door and blow his dirty little secret wide open.

I toss and turn that night enduring some of the worst nightmares I've experienced to date. Warren doesn't sleep much either, but I don't know if that's because he's nervous about breaking the law, or because I'm flailing around and keeping him awake. When dawn finally breaks, I stumble wearily downstairs and make myself a mug of extra strong coffee. Warren has finally dozed off, so I let him sleep for another hour before waking him. He yawns and stretches, then sits up and fumbles around for his phone. "I need to call the office and let them know I'll be coming in late."

"I'm relieved to hear you're not going to back out on me," I say. "I was afraid you might have changed your mind this morning."

He tightens his lips. "You can't breathe a word about this to anyone — not even to Amber. If it gets out that we were in the house, Gary could sue us for violation of privacy."

I arch a contemptuous brow at him. "And if we find Beth or Luna, or both of them, locked up in that room, you'd better believe the whole world's going to hear about it."

Warren pointedly ignores me and turns his attention to his phone.

I leave him to shower, and head back downstairs to scramble some eggs. We need to discuss the details of our plan over breakfast. I desperately want to be there when Warren removes the bedroom door, but it would be safer for both of us if I remain outside as the lookout in case Gary, or someone else, unexpectedly shows up at the house. As frustrating as it is, the only way to manage the situation safely is to divide and conquer.

I'm watching the butter sizzle in the pan when I hear Gary's car starting up next door. I throw down the spatula, dash to the family room, and watch until he turns the corner and disappears from sight. I check my watch and confirm that it's 7.15 a.m. — roughly the same time he takes off for work every morning. So far so good.

Twenty minutes later, Warren trudges into the kitchen looking as though he's carrying the weight of the world on his shoulders. "Maybe we shouldn't—"

"Don't start!" I cut him off. "We're not backing out now." I plop a plate of scrambled eggs and toast in front of him. "Coffee?"

He gives a sulky nod. "Was that Gary's car I heard pulling out?"

"Yes." I slide into the chair next to him and raise my mug to my lips. "I was thinking it might be best if I stayed outside as lookout while you're working on the door — just in case someone shows up."

Warren shovels a forkful of eggs in his mouth and grunts, presumably in agreement. He's not bailing on me, but he's clearly not happy about being strong-armed into my scheme.

"How long will it take you to remove the door?" I ask.

"Not long."

I raise my brows in an exasperated fashion. "How long is *not long*?"

He shoves his half-eaten plate of eggs to one side. "I don't know, Kay. It's not an exact science. I need to take a look at the door first. A few minutes, maybe. Depends how much jiggling I have to do. It's an older house, so the doors might stick."

I motion to his plate. "Are you done?"

"Yes." He stands abruptly, his chair scraping across the tile floor. "I'll go grab my tools."

Five minutes later, we're standing outside the back door of the rental. I feel like we're about to carry out a heist. Heart racing, I turn the key in the lock and nod to Warren. "Call me as soon as you have the door off."

He disappears inside with his tool bag, and I move to the side of the house, where I can keep an eye on anyone coming and going on the street. I shuffle from one foot to the other, checking my watch every few seconds to see how much time has elapsed. My mind conjures up every possible scenario of what could lie behind that bedroom door. When Maria Torres comes walking into view, I duck behind the trash cans until she passes. I don't want to be tied up in conversation with anyone when Warren calls.

Fifteen minutes go by, and there's still no word from him. I'm suddenly gripped by the panicked thought that Gary might be somewhere in the house lying in wait. I'm tempted to text Warren, but if he's wrestling with the door, he would have to drop everything to answer me.

At last, my phone chimes. "Did you get it off?" I ask in a breathless whisper.

"Yes," Warren replies. "You'd better come inside and take a look."

CHAPTER 31

I hurriedly stuff my phone back into my pocket and sprint around to the back door of the rental. After throwing a quick glance around, I slip inside and slam the door shut behind me. I can't shake the feeling that someone was watching me. But that's just me being paranoid. Not everyone hides behind their curtains spying on people like I do. Warren's right. Thanks to a potent combination of sleep deprivation and obsessive surveillance, my imagination is running rampant.

My pulse thuds in my ears as I race up the stairs as fast as I can possibly move, clinging to the railing for fear my legs will collapse beneath me. When I reach the landing, my eyes lock with Warren's, but I can't tell what emotion I'm reading in them. There's a strange flatness in his expression. Dread engulfs me, sending a wave of heat through my body. Are we too late to save them? I come to an abrupt halt, petrified of what I'm about to encounter: Beth, or Luna, on the verge of death, or worse — mummified corpses beneath the sheets. "Wh-what is it?" I stutter.

Warren gestures to the open doorway, inviting me to look for myself. I wish he would say something — anything. Is he in too much shock to speak? I'm not sure I want to see what he's seen. Reluctantly, I let go of the railing and trudge over to where he's standing, my legs twitching with every step.

I take a deep breath, then slowly survey the room, taking account of every detail. It doesn't take long. It's immaculate. Untouched. The guest bed is tastefully made up with crisp, white linens. The Target lamp I purchased sits atop the pine bedside locker I nabbed on Facebook marketplace for twenty bucks. I step inside the room, my gaze traveling around the serene space once more.

"Satisfied?" Warren asks in a wooden tone. I hear the disappointment in his voice — disappointment with me for leading him on this wild goose chase against his better judgement.

My throat feels dry. One by one, I pull open the drawers in the dresser but there's nothing in any of them. Kneeling down, I peek hesitantly under the bed. I can see through to the wall on the other side. I get to my feet in a daze, uncertain of how to process the scene. I was certain Gary was holding someone prisoner in here. Whoever moved that curtain had to have been locked in the room. It makes no sense.

"I don't understand," I say, wheeling around to face Warren. "Why did Gary put a lock on the door? There isn't even anything of value in here."

Warren tosses his screwdriver aside without meeting my eyes. "You'd better go outside and keep watch while I put this place back together."

I let out an indignant huff. "That's all you've got to say?"

"What do you want me to say, Kay?" He gives an all-too-familiar long-suffering shake of his head. "Your fantastical theories about our neighbor have no basis in reality. I don't know why he put a lock on the door — maybe he's planning to store something in here at some point. Granted, he should have asked permission, but at least he hasn't trashed the place, like some renters."

I narrow my eyes at Warren. "He doesn't get off the hook that easily. He could have moved Beth and cleaned up the room since yesterday. He put that lock on there for a reason, and if it's not to protect his stuff, then it was to keep someone imprisoned in here. I don't care what you say. He's taunting us. I think he did something to Beth and the whole rehab story was just a cover-up."

Warren shakes his head in disgust. "I've heard enough of your crazy talk. I did what you wanted. Now, let me get busy putting this door back where it belongs."

He sets his lips in a hard line and starts rummaging around in his tool bag.

I turn and stomp out of the room. Did Gary know I would try and sneak in here today? Just like he knew I would take a sample of the smoothie to be tested after Beth got out of the hospital. And just like he planted Maria's purse in the trash bag at the curb for me to find. He's always one step ahead of me. He knows I'm on to him, and he's deliberately misleading me. I need to find a way to gain the upper hand.

I'm standing at the side of the house, lost in my thoughts, when I hear Maria's frail voice call out to me. "Hello, Kay. Have you planted those seedlings I dropped off?" She's leaning over my garden wall, squinting into the flowerbeds.

I shoot Warren a quick text warning him not to come out yet, before walking over to Maria. "No, I haven't seen them. When did you drop them off?"

"I left them on your front doorstep yesterday. Lantanas and penstemons."

I blink, trying to think on my feet. Disappointment is etched on her face, so I smile warmly at her, despite the fore-boding feeling I have in my gut. "Warren probably put them in the potting shed and forgot to mention it. Thanks, Maria. I'll ask him about it when he gets home."

She bobs her head at me as she hobbles off. "Let me know if you'd like any more, dear."

The minute she's out of view, I dash to the green gar-bage can at the side of our house and peer inside it. A tray of smashed seedlings lies caked over the trash like chocolate frosting.

CHAPTER 32

It's been over a week since Luna supposedly went to visit her aunt in Portland, and she still hasn't resurfaced and her car hasn't moved. I'm not so sure that the woman Engelmann spoke to was Beth's sister. It could have been Luna pretending to be her. Or maybe I've got it all wrong, and Gary is holding Luna hostage someplace. Despite the lies she told about me to Officer Engelmann, I worry about her obsessively. Gary could have manipulated her into saying what she said. I can't imagine what his motive would be for abducting her — possibly financial? Maybe Luna stands in the way of Gary inheriting Beth's estate or a life insurance policy. The frustrating part is that I can't get the police to take any of my concerns seriously.

Warren is still upset with me for forcing him to trespass next door. Even though we weren't caught in the act, and there were no repercussions, it nags at him. He may be content not knowing why Gary installed a lock on the guest bedroom door, but I want answers. I've been thinking about hiring a private investigator to track down Beth's sister in Portland and find out if she's seen Luna recently. It's a drastic step, but it would be worth every penny if it allows me to sleep again. The skin beneath my eyes is sagging from too many restless nights with nightmares of a spectral Luna calling out to me for help.

Today is Saturday, and Amber is taking me shopping while Warren is off at a golf tournament. I desperately need to get out of the house and take a break from the insane merry-go-round I've been on. I'm spending all my time consumed by what's happening next door, and I've neglected Amber and ticked off Warren in the process. I made the mistake of telling him about the seedlings I found in the trash, and it ended up turning into a full-blown argument when I told him I suspected Gary was behind the sabotage. Warren even insinuated I might have done it myself to make Gary look bad. I can't believe our spat devolved into Warren defending a possible serial killer over his own wife.

I make a half-hearted effort to apply some concealer over the dark patches beneath my eyes while I wait for Amber to arrive — not that it does much to mask my haggard appearance. I feel as though I've aged a decade since the Finkels moved in on my world.

The doorbell chimes, jolting me out of my morbid thoughts. I hurry downstairs and greet Amber with a forced smile. "I'm ready. I'm just going to lock the back door and grab my purse."

"Take your time," she says, following me into the kitchen. "I see Gary's stepdaughter has returned."

"What?" I swing back around to face her. "When? Is Luna there now?"

Amber laughs. "Ease up on all the questions. I didn't actually see her, I just assumed she'd returned since her car is gone."

Shock detonates within me. How did I miss that? Luna must have come back from Portland in the middle of the night. Why didn't she let me know she was back? A feeling of unease creeps up my spine. Could Gary have moved Luna's car? Is he going to try and convince me that she came back under cover of darkness and drove off?

"Something doesn't feel right," I say, when I finally find my voice. "Luna would have come over to say goodbye to me before she took off."

Amber pouts her lips. "Why would you assume that? She didn't bother telling you she was going to Portland in the first place."

"Exactly," I say, snatching up my purse and heading to the front door. "Which is why I don't believe she ever left the house — at least, not of her own accord. And I don't think for a minute that she moved her own car."

Amber's eyes widen. "Do you think she's still next door?"

"Either that, or Gary moved her during the night."

"Risky," Amber muses, as we walk out to her Camry. "Carrying her out to a car parked at the curb, even at night. What if someone had seen him?"

"You're assuming he didn't chop her up or dissolve her in acid first."

Amber throws me an incredulous look. "Seriously, Kay? He's hardly Jeffrey Dahmer 2.0. Those nightmares are doing your head in. Maybe it's time you got a prescription for some sleeping pills."

We fall silent as she backs down the driveway. She's not wrong. I'm not thinking rationally anymore. My eyes sweep up and down the street on the off chance Amber might have been mistaken, but there's no sign of the silver Nissan that's been parked there for the past week. If Gary's gotten rid of Luna's car, it only heightens the likelihood that she's in serious danger.

Amber and I spend the next few hours wandering through clothing stores searching for an outfit for me to wear to an upcoming wedding. I try on several different styles at Amber's behest, but my heart's not in the process. She pokes and prods at me, cajoling me to commit to one of the dresses, but when I look at myself in the mirror, all I can see are the faces of the two women who've gone missing, pleading with me to help find them.

CHAPTER 33

I finally purchase a mediocre-looking navy dress just to end the agony of having to try on any more ensembles. I'll probably end up taking the dress back, but Amber doesn't need to know that. She's been working double time to find me something suitable to wear to the wedding and she's delighted that I've finally settled on one of her suggestions. Shopping bags in tow, we head up to the food court in the mall and carry our trays to an open table.

"I think you made a good choice going with the navy dress," Amber says, stabbing her plastic fork into a piece of orange chicken. "It's elegant without being too showy — the kind of dress you can wear more than once."

"Uh-huh," I mumble, barely paying attention as she rambles on.

She stops chewing and peers at me intently. "Did you even hear a word I said?"

"Yes, sorry. Great dress. I'm a little distracted."

"Is it the Luna thing?"

I set down my fork and push my plate aside. "I'm thinking about hiring a PI to find out where she is. I just need to know that she's safe. She was scared of Gary that night we talked at my house. I can't rule out the possibility that he's done something to her."

Amber lets out an exasperated sigh. "You said that police officer — Engelmann, I think was his name — spoke to her. He told you she's fine. You have to drop this, Kay. Luna's not your ongoing responsibility."

"I don't agree. I shared my suspicions with her that Gary might have done something to her mother. If she confronted him about it, he could have decided to shut her up. I meddled in the situation, and I might have made things worse for her. Now her car has mysteriously disappeared. The least I can do is try to locate her and make sure nothing's happened. If I hire a PI and find out Gary is lying about her being in Portland, the police will be obligated to do something."

Amber peels the paper from her straw and sticks it in her water. "I think you're getting ahead of yourself with the whole private investigator thing. There could be a perfectly simple explanation for why Luna's car's gone. Maybe she's back from Portland and drove into town or something."

I throw her a doubtful look as I sip my lemonade. The likelihood that Luna arrived back from Portland in the middle of the night and took off into town early this morning is slim to none. But Amber's right. Hiring a PI is a last resort. First, I need to question Gary and hear what he has to say about the Nissan being gone. And I'll hit him up about the seedlings I found in the trash while I'm at it. I know he tossed them — he's goading me. Not to mention the fact that he hates Maria and would never pass up an opportunity to spite her.

Back at the house, I resume my demented pacing behind the family room curtains watching for Gary's return. It's not a workday, so he could show up at any minute, and I can't afford to miss his arrival. If I fail to intercept him before he goes into the house, I know he won't answer the door to me.

It's mid-afternoon before I spot his green BMW turning onto the street. I bolt outside and wait for him to pull into the driveway before approaching the car.

He scowls as he climbs out. "Is there a problem?" he asks, his tone so icy it's jarring.

I glower back at him. "Why did you throw my seedlings in the trash?"

He wrinkles his brow. "What seedlings?"

"Don't play games with me. The ones Maria left at my front door yesterday."

Gary lets out an impatient snort. "I have no idea what you're talking about. Now, if you'll excuse me, I have things to do."

He tries to walk around me, but I take a quick step to the side to block him. "How about Luna's car — the silver Nissan that's been parked at the curb for the past week? Where is it?"

"What are you? The HOA police? Get out of my way!"

His tone has taken on a menacing edge, but I refuse to be intimidated. I don't yield my position, forcing him to step onto the lawn to get around me.

"I know Luna's not in Portland," I say. "I'm going to report her missing. And if the police don't do anything about it, I'll hire a PI to find her if I have to."

Gary raises a condescending eyebrow at me as though I'm a child who has disappointed him. "Do you really think the cops will take you seriously after so many false alarms?"

"Yes," I retort. "Now that Luna's car's missing, it changes everything."

He sneers at me, a dangerous glint in his eye. "I'll spare you from making a fool of yourself to the cops again. If you must know, I sold the car at Luna's request. She's decided to stay in Portland."

CHAPTER 34

Gary's latest trumped-up story about selling Luna's car has only made me more determined than ever to find her and get to the bottom of what's going on. I spend the next couple of days researching reputable PIs online. After perusing the websites and reading the reviews, I pull the trigger on hiring George Barlow, a middle-aged, soft-spoken man who charges a reasonable rate and promises to get back to me within forty-eight hours. I'm not able to give him a whole lot of information, other than Beth's and Luna's names, and Gary's details from the rental application, but George assures me it should be enough to track down Luna's aunt.

I'm bitterly disappointed when he calls me back the following day with the news that he's been unable to locate any living relatives of a Beth Finkel in the Portland area.

"I'm sure Beth told me her sister lived there," I say.

"I can't find any trace of her," George replies. "And the previous addresses you gave me from the rental paperwork don't check out for either Beth or Gary Finkel. Or Beth Webster — you had mentioned Luna's surname was Webster, so I thought it was worth checking out. Do you happen to know Beth's maiden name?"

"No. I didn't know her very long before she disappeared."

"I wish I could give you better news, but I'm afraid I can't help you any further at this time," George says. "It's a dead end. Feel free to call me back if you get ahold of any more information."

I hang up feeling frustrated and at a total loss as to what to do next. The only thing I know for sure is that I'm not ready to give up. I have to find out what happened to my neighbor and her daughter — for my own sanity, if for no other reason. It's possible Gary did sell Luna's car. There's no point in him keeping it if he's gotten rid of her. I browse around online for a while trying to figure out if there's a way to track down the sale. Apparently, I need a VIN to get any information. I trawl through several online sites, including Facebook marketplace, but I don't see Luna's silver Nissan listed for sale or marked as sold. If I could find out who bought the car, I could ask them what Gary told them about the previous owner. I strongly suspect it won't jive with the story he told me about Luna visiting her aunt. The discrepancy might be enough to pique the police's interest.

Over dinner, I'm quieter than usual, but Warren is still too miffed with me to care. Eventually, he sets down his fork with a clatter. "All right, what's bothering you now?"

I flatten my lips in a tight line. "Our neighbor, what else?"

"What's he been doing, other than absconding with his family members?"

"It's not funny, Warren."

He blows out a heavy breath. "Someone needs to lighten the mood around here. You've convinced yourself of the most harrowing explanation without a shred of evidence to back it up. I'm sure Luna will show up any day now, safe and sound, after spending some healing time reminiscing about her mother with her aunt. Regardless, I've decided not to renew Gary's lease when it's up. Until then, we're stuck with him. Now, can we please talk about something else?"

"Fine. Did you happen to see the seedlings Maria left for me by the front door last week? I meant to ask you about them and I forgot."

He scratches his forehead as though flummoxed by the seemingly inane change of subject. "No, I can't say I did."

"I found them in our trash can."

Warren frowns. "I'm confused. So, Maria *didn't* leave them by the front door?"

"She did. What I'm telling you is that someone tossed them into our trash." I arch a meaningful brow at him. "If it wasn't you, and it wasn't me, I wonder who it could have been?"

A flash of irritation crosses Warren's face. "Let's not go there again. What interest would Gary Finkel have in throwing away your seedlings?"

"I think he's messing with me."

"O-kay." Warren eyes me uncertainly. "And why is he messing with you?"

"I haven't figured that out yet. But he's definitely behind it. And I know it was him who put Maria's purse in the trash by the curb the day after she reported it missing. I'm not sure if he was trying to pin the theft on me or Beth."

Warren places his hands on his head. "Stop! *Please!* You've got to drop this, Kay. You have zero evidence that Gary's behind any of this, whatever *this* is. I'm serious, the neighbors are beginning to talk."

I freeze, my fork halfway to my lips. "What do you mean?"

"They're not sure you should be heading up the HOA anymore. They all know you hang out behind the curtains with your binoculars, spying on people — you think you're such a good sleuth, but they've seen you skulking around. Everyone agrees you do a great job organizing neighborhood events and such, but you take things to an extreme when it comes to sticking your nose in where it doesn't belong."

I fold my arms in front of me, my blood boiling at the thought of the neighbors talking to Warren about me behind my back. "Like what?"

"Like thinking Gary Finkel is some kind of serial killer. You've been spreading rumors about him, and you're scaring people."

"I'm just looking out for everyone else on the street," I retort. "He might be dangerous. It's better to warn people so they can take precautions."

"Folks here don't want the neighborhood getting a bad name, Kay. It's not good for property prices. They also don't like the fact that you call out the police for insignificant reasons."

"It looked like a break-in was taking place if that's what you're talking about. I didn't know he'd locked himself out. What am I supposed to do, ignore suspicious activity when I see it?"

Warren reaches for my hands and looks earnestly into my eyes. "That's exactly what I want you to do. Promise me from now on that you'll stay away from Gary Finkel and out of his business."

CHAPTER 35

Despite Warren's impassioned plea, the last thing I'm going to do is stay away from Gary Finkel. I'm watching him more closely than ever. I don't care if people think I'm the strange one. Maybe I am being paranoid, but it seems to me as though he's growing more shifty by the day — peering over his shoulder when he exits the house, coming and going at odd hours, carrying black trash bags in and out to his car. It's all very Dahmer-esque. All the peculiarities are starting to form a disturbing pattern. He could easily be disposing of body parts and dropping them off at various dumpsters. I'm certain Warren would have the same qualms about our renter's behavior if he could see what I see.

Despite numerous attempts by the other neighbors on the street to engage Gary, he keeps to himself and makes no attempt to interact with any of them. The official line is still that Beth is in rehab, but rumors of her passing are spreading, and I'm no longer denying them. Warren, on the other hand, keeps making excuses for Gary's behavior. He thinks we need to show him some grace while he's still in mourning. What a joke! It was obvious there was no love lost between Gary and Beth.

Everything I witnessed about their relationship only confirmed my impression that Gary was abusing Beth. The malicious glint in his eyes, fueled by intoxication from the power he exuded over her. All her mannerisms projected despair: her constant hand wringing, her dejected tone of voice, her slouched posture — a woman worn down by a domineering husband. It raises the question: how far did he take things? Could he really be a killer? I'm tempted to call George back and have him investigate Gary a little deeper. Beth mentioned that he'd been married before. Perhaps George could find out who Gary's first wife is, and whether she's still alive. I mull it over for only a minute or two before dialing the PI's number.

"Kay, I take it you have some new information for me?" George says.

"Not exactly. I need you to go in another direction and do some digging into Gary's past. He was married before he met Beth. I want to know if his first wife is still alive. If so, I'll need her contact information."

George gives a polite cough. "And if she's not?"

"Then I need to know how she died."

There's a long pause before George responds. "I can guess where you're going with this. You want to know if there's a chance that Gary killed his first wife."

I let out a fluttery breath. "If he did it once, he might do it again."

"Have you talked to the police at all about your neighbor's disappearance?"

"Yes, but they can't act on a hunch that something's amiss. Unless there's evidence of foul play, they say there's nothing they can do. They can't even search his house without probable cause. But, if it turns out his first wife disappeared, or died under mysterious circumstances, they might be willing to take a closer look."

"I'll jump on it as soon as I can," George promises. "It might be a few days before you hear back from me. I've got a couple of clients ahead of you."

"Do you need anything else from me?" I ask. "I don't have any new information, other than what Gary listed on the rental paperwork I sent over."

"I'll start with that," George says. "I'll be in touch."

I hang up and let out a sigh of relief. He didn't make any promises, but having him on board is better than nothing. If Gary's first wife is alive, she might be able to shed some light on things. And if she's deceased, the circumstances surrounding her death might be very revealing.

I'm in need of some fresh air to clear my head, so I retire to the backyard to tackle some long overdue weeding. I've just come out of the garden shed after donning my gloves when I notice a handwritten sign of some sort in Gary's upstairs guest bedroom window. I make my way over to the gate between our backyards to get close enough to read it.

My heart begins to jackhammer in my chest. I stare at the sign in disbelief, then pull off my gardening gloves and rub my eyes to make sure I'm not hallucinating. But when I look up again, the sign is still there.

Help me!

The breath leaves my lungs. Someone's in there — someone who needs help. I knew that room was designed to be a prison. There was no other explanation for that deadbolt. Tossing my gloves onto a patio chair, I dash into the house to call 911. But something makes me hesitate. Now that I'm back in the safety of my kitchen, I'm second-guessing myself. It's not the first time I've conjured something up in my mind that isn't there. Did I actually see a sign? I press my fingers to my temples. *Yes!* It was definitely there. I didn't imagine it, did I?

I sprint back out to the backyard, phone in hand to snap a picture, but when I look up at the bedroom window, the sign is gone.

CHAPTER 36

This can't be happening. I know I didn't imagine the *help me* sign in the window. The words were written on some kind of fabric — a bedsheet, maybe a T-shirt — in bold, red paint. I swallow the lump in my throat. I assumed it was paint — except where would Luna get paint from if she's locked in a bedroom? I quash the uncomfortable thought that she might have deliberately cut herself to write that cry for help. There are other possibilities, like lipstick. I pace across the room, one hand on my hip, debating with myself. Did I see a message because I wanted to — a subliminal permission slip of sorts to go back inside Gary's house? Visualization is a powerful thing. I can't rule out the possibility that my mind is playing tricks on me. Do I really believe that Luna is a prisoner next door and not safely ensconced in her aunt's house in Portland flipping through old photo albums of her mother?

If I did see a message in the window, why did Luna take it down? Was she afraid Gary would discover it before she was rescued? I'm itching to call Warren and tell him about it, but I won't be able to talk him into going back over to Gary's place with me again now that the sign's gone. Maybe Amber would. I dial her number, but it goes straight to voicemail. A moment later, I get a text.

At the dentist. What's up?

I hesitate before messaging her back. She might alert Warren if I tell her what I'm up to.

All good, just wanted to catch up.

Pocketing my phone, I take a deep breath. If I'm going to do this, I'm on my own. I can't in good conscience do nothing. I can't unsee what I saw — or think I saw. The least I can do is go next door and knock on the bedroom door again. If Luna's there, maybe she'll answer me this time. That's all it would take for me to call 911 and unleash the full power of the law on Gary Finkel. I haven't forgotten the pleading look in Beth's eyes the first time I met her. Maybe I didn't keep the promise I made to myself that day to help her, but I can still save her daughter.

My phone chimes and I glance at it distractedly. It's Amber again.

Sure you're OK? Want me to call you when I'm done here?

I tap out a quick reply. *No need, busy with work. Catch you later.*

I unlock my phone for easy access and turn it on silent, then retrieve the key to the rental from the rack in the mudroom. Maybe I should bring some tools with me in case this turns into a hostage rescue situation. I hurry back out to the garden shed and run an appraising eye over Warren's impressive array of cordless drills, saws, and grinders. Who am I kidding? I don't even know how to turn these tools on, let alone operate them. I'm not going to waste time trying to figure out how to take the door off its hinges. If Gary's holding someone prisoner in there, I'll break the door down to get them out. I set my phone on the workbench and reach for the sledgehammer in the corner of the shed. After swinging it back and forth a couple of times to make sure I can handle it, I proceed across the lawn to the rental. The sledgehammer is considerably heavier than I anticipated. Hopefully, I can wield it effectively if I have to. I'm trusting the adrenaline shooting through me will give me a much-needed boost in the moment.

I cast an anxious glance over my shoulder as I unlock the back door and slip inside Gary's house once more. It's eerily quiet inside, a mausoleum of sorts. Oddly vacant of Beth's presence. A sense of outrage simmers in my gut. Granted, she was a mess, but no one deserved to be treated the way she was — broken down and stripped of her dignity. I reach for the sledgehammer and make my way to the stairs, stopping briefly to listen for any signs of movement on the upper level.

With each step, my dread mounts. I feel like I'm starring in some kind of horror movie, dragging a sledgehammer behind me as I march toward an unsuspecting victim asleep in their bed. The hammer grows weightier by the minute. I was kidding myself to think I would have the strength to brandish it as a weapon if Gary were suddenly to materialize in front of me. I'm kicking myself now for not bringing the gun from our safe instead.

I stop at the top of the stairs to catch my breath. The bedroom doors are all closed and a dreadful sense of déjà vu sets in. The drums of war beat in my chest as I anticipate what could be waiting for me. What if I'm making a terrible mistake, and Gary's leading me into a trap?

CHAPTER 37

I feel like a disembodied spirit as I force my legs to start moving in the direction of the guest bedroom. Tightening my fingers around the handle of the sledgehammer, I come to a halt in front of the door. I throw a tentative glance around, half-expecting Gary to burst through it, foam dripping from his mouth as he lunges toward me with a raised knife. It's the fantastical stuff of my nightmares, but I can't shake the image from my mind. Maybe I'm being paranoid, but I'm convinced he's a psychopath, even if Warren has fallen for his lies. After all, psychopaths can present as normal until they elect to show their true colors.

I'm vibrating with fear as I raise my fist and knock. "Luna, are you in there?" I press my ear to the door, then repeat the question, shouting this time as I rap my knuckles harder on the wood.

Silence echoes down the hallway. I try to visualize the sign I saw in the window, but the image is already fading. I can't trust my own memory. I'm too sleep-deprived to know what's real and what isn't anymore. Disheartened, I reach for the sledgehammer, but as I turn to go back down the stairs, my ears pick up on a faint muttering on the other side of the door. I freeze and spin back around just as a weak voice breaks the silence: "Hello? Is someone there?"

My heart rushes up my throat at the sound of Luna's voice. I drop the hammer and slap frantic palms on the door. "Luna! It's me, Kay. I'm going to get you out of there. Stand back. I brought a sledgehammer."

"Wait! There's a key up above on the door frame," she replies.

I drop the hammer back down with a *thunk* and feel around with my fingers along the top of the dusty door frame until they curl around a small metal key. "Found it!"

I jam the key in the lock, then wrench the door open. I come to an abrupt halt, paralyzed by shock. A disheveled, wide-eyed Luna stares back at me. Her hands are bound, and her feet are leashed to a bedpost with a rope with enough slack to allow her to move around. A gag, that she's somehow managed to work free, hangs around her neck.

When I recover from the shock, I dash across to her and begin trying to loosen the bonds on her wrists. "Did Gary do this to you?" I mutter, through gritted teeth.

"Yes. He's insane," she sobs. "I think he killed my mom."

"Everything's going to be okay. You're safe now," I assure her. "I'll call 911 as soon as I untie you." Even as the words leave my mouth, I suddenly remember that I've left my phone in the garden shed. Calling for help will have to wait until we are safely out of here. I wrestle with the rope for a few more minutes but it's impossible to loosen it. "I need to run down to the kitchen and get a knife," I tell Luna. "I can't get this knot undone."

Her shoulders sag, an air of hopelessness clouding her countenance. "What if he comes back?"

"All the more reason to get out of here as quickly as possible, but I can't free you without a knife." I grip her by the shoulders and look her directly in her eyes. "I'll come right back. I promise I won't leave you here."

Before she can argue with me any further, I sprint from the room, taking the stairs two at a time in a mad dash to the kitchen. Eying the butcher block on the counter, I select the most menacing-looking knife and run back upstairs, praying I don't trip en route and stab myself in the heart. Not the smartest move to run with a serrated blade, but this constitutes an emergency.

The relief on Luna's pale face is palpable when I get back to the room. I drop to my knees next to her and begin sawing at the rope around her wrists. "What was Gary planning to do with you?" I ask, heartened to see the rope begin to fray under my efforts.

"I don't know. He said he had something special planned for me, but he needed to make preparations first." Her voice breaks. "All I did was ask him for the phone number for the rehab facility Mom was in. He went ballistic — he told me I stood to inherit nothing, and that she'd written me out of her will." She gulps back a sob. "I don't care about the money. I was just devastated that I never got to say goodbye or tell her how sorry I was for how I treated her."

The rope finally snaps, and Luna exhales in relief as she rubs her wrists. I'm halfway through sawing the rope on her ankles when I hear an unwelcome sound behind me.

I spin around to meet Gary's dark probing eyes, emanating pure hatred.

CHAPTER 38

I scramble to my feet, still clutching the knife, but freeze when I see Gary reach for the sledgehammer by the door. He swings it menacingly backward and forward. "You just couldn't keep your nose out of it, could you?" he seethes.

"It's over," I tell him. "You need to turn yourself in to the police and confess to whatever it is you did to Beth."

He throws back his head and laughs, a harsh menacing sound that fills me with trepidation. It's not the sound of someone who's afraid. It's the sick, raucous sound of someone who's confident he's in total control of the situation. "And what exactly is it that you think I did to Beth?" he asks, sounding amused.

"I don't know for sure. But I do know she didn't go to rehab. I called around a bunch of places and no one has heard of her."

Gary raises an eyebrow. "Maybe you didn't call the right place. Or maybe I admitted her under a false name. Or perhaps they were lying to you because they don't give out medical information to nosy strangers."

"If you had nothing to hide, you would have given Luna the information she asked for. She has a right to know what happened to her mother."

Gary scowls. "She gave up that right a long time ago."

"You can't keep her here. She's coming with me. Step aside," I say, hoping he can't detect the waver in my voice.

"I'm the one giving orders in this house," he snarls. "Drop the knife and kick it over to me."

I hesitate, gripping the handle more tightly. I'm reluctant to give it up, even though I'm not sure I could bring myself to stab him.

He raises the sledgehammer, resting the metal head in his left hand. "I'll count to five, then I'm going to test my swing on someone's kneecap. Eeny, meeny, miny, moe."

Luna yelps and tries to scoot backward. She hugs her knees to her chest, her ankles still partially bound with the rope. Her defeated posture tells me she's not going to fight her way out of here alongside me. I can't risk Gary seriously injuring her. Grimacing, I drop the knife and kick it across the floor, my hope plummeting when he picks it up with a contemptuous curl of his lips. Maybe, between the two of us, Luna and I could have overpowered him, but if it's just me against him, I don't have a hope of prevailing.

He fishes several zip ties out of his pocket and walks over to me brandishing the knife to my throat. "Turn around."

I have no option but to comply. I wince as he yanks the zip ties tight, then shoves me to the floor and secures my ankles to a bedpost with a rope. He repeats the process with Luna, who sobs quietly throughout. My heart breaks for her. I offered her a smidgen of hope and now he's snatched it from her again.

"Where's your phone?" Gary asks.

"In our garden shed," I say.

He eyes me skeptically, then pulls out his own phone and dials. When it goes to voicemail he ends the call, then pats me down roughly, presumably to make sure I don't have my phone on silent.

Without another word, he backs out of the room, slams the door, and locks it behind him. My heart shudders almost to a halt in my chest, but I can't let Luna think I've given up. "We need to make a plan before he comes back," I say, lowering my voice on the off chance he's listening outside the door, or possibly even recording us. "There's two of us against one of him, so we have that advantage, at least."

She gives a despairing shake of her head. "There's nothing we can do. He's armed. We have no way of gaining the upper hand."

"That's not true. He's got to be vulnerable at times. Does he bring you food regularly?"

She dips her head in a tearful nod. "Once or twice a day."

"There you go. We'll surprise him when his hands are full."

Luna looks at me like I'm talking gibberish. "How are we supposed to do that with our wrists and ankles zip tied?"

I scoot closer to her. "I haven't figured that part out yet, but I will." I get to work painstakingly trying to pick the frayed ends of the rope apart. "I saw your sign in the window."

Luna wrinkles her brow. "What sign?"

I stop what I'm doing and gawp at her. "You're kidding, right? You put a *help me* sign in the window. It looked like it was written on a sheet, or an old T-shirt or something." I throw a quick glance around the room. "What did you do with it? Did you hide it under the mattress?"

Luna stares at me, jaw askew. "Gary was at the window when I woke up earlier. I thought I saw him shoving something into his pocket." She hesitates. "He must have put the sign up. That means . . ." Her voice trails off.

"That means he lured me here," I say in a wooden tone. I scrunch my eyes shut and groan. He knew I would fall into his trap. How could I have been so stupid? I should have seen it coming.

CHAPTER 39

Gary knew I was closing in on him — sharing my suspicions with the police and threatening to hire a PI to investigate him. He knew I wouldn't give up until I got answers. He had to do something to stop me. A shiver goes down my spine. He can't let me go now. He's in too deep. I'm about to meet the same fate as Beth. I grit my teeth as I tug helplessly at the zip ties around my wrists.

Gary's crazy if he thinks he can get away with this. He can't keep me locked up next door to my own home and think no one's going to find out about it. My car is parked in the garage. Warren will report me missing when he gets home from work and can't get ahold of me. He'll find my phone in the garden shed and notice that the sledgehammer is gone from its usual spot — he's fastidious about his tools. After everything that's gone down, he'll know who's behind my disappearance. The police will have probable cause to enter Gary's house, and they'll haul him off in handcuffs the minute they discover me and Luna locked inside this room. Despite my logical progression of thought, I'm not in the least bit reassured by my own reasoning. I've already concluded that Gary's a psychopath, and psychopaths are cunning.

A small sob interrupts my musing. I scoot over to Luna, curled up in a fetal position on the floor, and gently pull the hair back from her face. Her cheeks are wet with tears. "I'm going to get us out of here," I say. "But you have to stay strong. I need you to tell me everything that's happened since I last saw you."

She furrows her brow, as though considering where to start. "I tried to be amicable, at first. I thought Gary might be more open to giving me information if I didn't confront him. But he threatened to kick me out of the house the minute I started asking questions. That's when I told him you'd offered me a place to stay, and that you'd shared your suspicions with me about what happened to my mom. His demeanor changed right away. I think he slipped something into my drink after that. Next thing I know, I'm waking up in a bathroom, tied to the pedestal sink. Later on, he moved me in here."

"What has he told you about your mother?"

Luna sniffs and wipes the back of her hands over her eyes before sitting up. "Nothing. He wouldn't tell me anything about her last days, or what happened at the rehab facility. He said I didn't deserve to know after turning my back on her. He said . . . he said she hated me."

"That's not true," I interject. "I know for a fact that Beth adored you. She was brokenhearted about your estrangement. She wanted nothing more than to reconnect with you, but she didn't know where you were."

Luna's expression darkens. "I emailed her my address, but I never heard back from her. Gary must have deleted it. All this time, I thought she didn't want to patch things up with me."

"Gary's been gaslighting your mother ever since they moved in next door. He told me about her past addiction issues. He made out she was severely depressed and under psychiatric care. To be honest, she did seem out of it a lot of the time — forgetful and confused — but I'm pretty sure he was drugging her and spreading rumors about her abusing prescription pills. He even told me she was prosecuted in the past for shoplifting to feed her drug habit. Next thing you know, my neighbor's purse was stolen out of her house during our annual block party. Gary pretended to be outraged when I asked him if Beth could have taken it, but I think he set the whole thing up to frame her."

Luna frowns. "Are you talking about Maria Torres?"

I eye her curiously. "Yes, how do you know her?"

"I don't — not really. She came over to see Gary the first night I was here, and I overheard the conversation. She was giving out to him about how he'd treated my mom at the block party. And then she scolded him about some argument he had outside her house late one night. She threatened to report him to the police for assaulting his wife. She also mentioned something about her purse being stolen and how things like that never happened until he showed up. He was furious when she left — beet red and ranting about how he'd like to rip off every one of her scrawny limbs."

I gasp in alarm at the thought of Gary physically harming Maria. I doubt it's an idle threat. He made one woman disappear and took another hostage; he can do it again. I need to find a way to get out of here and warn Maria that she's in danger.

"Has Gary been keeping you prisoner in here the whole time?" I ask.

Luna shakes her head. "No, I've been in his bathroom most of the time. He made me sleep in the tub. He kept me tied up and drugged until last night when he moved me in here."

"How do you know he's been drugging you?"

She gives a scoffing laugh. "He told me so. He's proud of it. He forces me to drink this green smoothie he brings me. There's nothing I can do to stop him with my hands tied."

My stomach churns. I have every reason to believe Gary will try the same thing with me. And if I'm drugged, he can ferry me out of the house in the middle of the night, just like I suspect he did with Beth, and no one will ever know.

Somehow, I have to keep believing we'll find a way to get out of here before that happens.

"Warren will call the police when he gets home from work and finds me missing," I say to Luna, more to convince myself than anything else. Warren might work late tonight. What if he decides to wait until morning before filing a missing person's report? What if he comes over here by himself to look for me, and Gary overpowers him — or worse, kills him? I squeeze my hands into fists. I need to stop my dire thoughts from spiraling any further.

"Even if the police show up at the door, Gary can talk his way out of anything," Luna says.

I chew on my lip. She's not wrong. He's fooled the police before. He lied successfully to Engelmann.

"Were you ever in Portland visiting your aunt?" I ask.

Luna throws me a befuddled look. "What are you talking about? I told you, I've been locked up here the whole time."

"So you never spoke to the police — an officer called Engelmann?"

Luna rolls her eyes. "If I had, I'd hardly be tied up in this bedroom right now, would I? Why are you asking me this?"

"I tried to alert the police to the fact that you were missing under suspicious circumstances. They talked to Gary, and he gave them your aunt's number in Portland. At least that's what he told them. Officer Engelmann reported back to me that he'd spoken to you."

Luna lets out a disconcerted huff. "And you believed him?"

I shrug. "He gave me details of our conversation, so I had no reason to doubt it was you. Now I realize Gary took what you told him and fed it to whomever his cohort was on the other end of the phone pretending to be you and your aunt."

I freeze at the sound of the door unlocking. Seconds later, Gary steps into the room holding a tumbler in his hand. My skin prickles with fear. He's moving more quickly than I anticipated. If he spirits me out of here before Warren returns home from work, it's likely no one will ever find me.

CHAPTER 40

When I come to, it takes me a minute to remember what happened. I have a fuzzy recollection of Gary yanking my head back by my hair and forcing some vile, green liquid down my throat. I groan as I rearrange my limbs from the cramped position I'm lying in on the floor. Slowly, I get to my feet and sit on the edge of the bed. I'm surprised to see that Gary hasn't moved me out of the bedroom yet. I lift my head and glance around the oddly quiet space. My heart slugs against my chest when I realize what's different. Luna is gone!

I take a few short, stabbing breaths, trying not to panic. Where has Gary taken her? I kick at the bedpost in frustration, trying in vain to wrestle my feet free. I wanted to rescue Luna, but what if I've made things worse for her? I might have pushed Gary into getting rid of her. Tears prickle my eyes. I should have called the police right away and told them about the message in the window — or gone to the media with my story — whatever it took to convince someone that Gary was holding his stepdaughter against her will. Coming over here on a wing and a prayer, with a sledgehammer I could barely lift, was the dumbest idea of all. Not to mention the fact that I left my phone and gun behind. Evidently, I'm not cut out for vigilante justice.

I glance helplessly at the window. I could yell for help, but who's going to hear me through the double glazing and heavy drapes muffling the sound? Exasperated, I try to yank my wrists free. A pathetic gesture, but infinitely more satisfying than sitting here waiting on a monster to decide my fate.

My stomach growls and I wonder if Gary will bring me any food. Not likely, if he's planning on killing me anyway. I have no idea what time it is, or how many hours I've been passed out cold. Does Warren realize yet that I'm missing? If he's home, he must have discovered my phone in the shed by now. He'll see that the gate leading into Gary's backyard is open and he'll know where I am. Maybe he's already come over to ask Gary if he's seen me. A jolt of fear goes through me. What if Gary whacked him on the back of the head and dragged him into the house before he even realized what was happening?

I groan at the thought. I need to stop thinking this way. It accomplishes nothing. My best hope of getting out of here is to try and reason with Gary to let me go. But what can I possibly say to convince him? I know too much now.

I almost jump out of my skin when I hear the key turning in the lock again. I scoot back, tensing when the door flings open. My jaw drops when Luna walks into the room carrying a sandwich on a plastic tray. She keeps her eyes downcast, but I can see that her face is horribly battered and bruised. Gary hovers a step behind her, steering her by clamping her elbow, just like he used to do with Beth. Luna shuffles toward me and lowers the tray as though to set it on the bed.

"Not there!" Gary snaps. "Leave it on the floor. She can eat like the dog she is."

Luna dutifully moves away from the bed and kneels down to set the tray on the floor.

"You'd better not be trying to signal for help," Gary says, striding over to the window. He pulls one of the drapes aside and peeks out, then checks all around and beneath the sill, presumably for a makeshift sign.

I slide off the bed and crouch down next to Luna. "I'm so sorry he did this to you," I whisper.

Eyes fastened like leeches on Gary's back, she deftly slides a steak knife from her sleeve and slips it beneath the tray. Wordlessly, she gets to her feet just as Gary turns around and walks back over to us. He scowls down at me. "You have Luna to thank for your last meal. Enjoy it while you can."

"You won't get away with this," I say, hating the fact that my chin is wobbling. "I'm sure Warren has reported me missing by now. The police will be here any minute. It will be better for you if you let me go before they get here."

Gary throws back his head and laughs. "I hate to burst your bubble, but Warren the Toolman won't be showing up here any time soon. He isn't the superhero you think he is. He's currently wallowing in a pool of his own blood, the unwitting victim of a home invasion." A satisfied smile flicks across Gary's lips. "Shame how the neighborhood has gone to pot lately. First, it was that old hag's purse, now it's robbery and deadly assault at the home of the HOA president."

CHAPTER 41

Shock prickles over my clammy skin. *No!* It can't be true. Warren always chided me for jumping straight to the worst-case scenario, and now he's become the embodiment of it. I don't understand how Gary was able to stage a home invasion without anyone hearing or seeing a thing. I bury my face in my hands as the full horror of the situation hits me. My husband has been brutally attacked; he might be dead. I knew Gary was evil — a serial killer, even — but just how many people has he killed? If he's gone this far, he won't hesitate to add me to the list. And now I'm trapped here. I was counting on Warren to raise the alarm — a false hope, as it turns out. He needs rescuing as much as I do. "Is my husband still alive?" I manage to squeak out.

Gary smirks. "If he is, he won't last long. He's bleeding like a stuck pig."

"You're sick and twisted!" I yell. "You need to call for an ambulance right now. It might not be too late to save him."

Gary gives a sly grin. "I have a feeling that window of opportunity's closed. Home invasions nowadays are a nasty business. These people don't mess around. They don't want any witnesses."

"The police will start looking for me as soon as Warren's body is discovered," I say, trying not to cry as my voice wavers.

Gary rubs a hand over the dark stubble on his chin. "They're not going to be looking for you here. They'll think you've been taken by the same people who broke into your house."

Desperation surges through my veins. I need to get away from this madman. My eyes flick to the tray of food on the floor, and then to Luna. She gives a subtle shake of her head. Now is not the time to lunge at Gary with the knife when he can easily fend off the attack. I need to undo my bonds first, then catch him unawares when he's coming through the door, or when he's at the window with his back turned to me.

He grabs Luna roughly by the arm and shoves her toward the door.

"Leave her with me!" I yell. "She's done nothing to you. You've taken everything from her already."

He lets out a snide chuckle as he strides through the door and slams it behind him. The sound reverberates around inside my head. The lock turns, and any last remaining hope of intervening in Gary's plans for Luna fades. I can't believe she had the wherewithal to slip me a knife. I don't know where she found the courage. She was falling apart earlier, but something inspired her to take a chance.

I slide the steak knife out from underneath the tray and get to work sawing at the zip ties on my wrists. It's a delicate process as I can't see what I'm doing, but the blade is surprisingly sharp and makes short work of my bonds. I tackle the rope around my ankles next and, the minute I'm free, I dash to the window. I'm afraid to start banging on the glass and yelling in case Gary comes back. Who would hear me anyway? I could try and make some kind of makeshift sign, but I have nothing to write with. I glance at the knife I'm holding, but the thought of drawing blood makes me physically sick. I've never been good with gore at the best of times. If I pass out now, I might miss the opportunity to surprise Gary and make my escape.

I'm certain Luna didn't give me the knife just so I could free myself. She's counting on me to neutralize Gary and free her from his clutches. I sink down on the bed and think about how best to go about trying to overpower him. Jumping him when the door opens again is not ideal — Luna might come through first and I can't risk injuring her. I like my chances better when he's at the window with his back turned to me. That way, I can stab him and make a dash for the door, and hopefully lock him in before he rallies enough to come after me.

I swallow hard at the thought of plunging a knife into human flesh. I'm not sure I can do it. But then my thoughts turn to Warren. I can't imagine the shock he must have felt when Gary attacked him. If there's even the smallest chance that he's clinging to life next door — unconscious but breathing — I have to do whatever it takes to get out of here and help him. Surely someone will find him soon. Maybe they've already raised the alarm. Gary said he staged a home invasion, which means the front door is likely lying open. Someone is bound to investigate when they see it. Maria passes by our house every day on her daily loop around the neighborhood. I grimace at the thought of my elderly neighbor finding Warren. She's been through enough already without the added trauma of discovering my husband lying in a pool of blood. More important, I'm worried about her safety. Gary would delight in taking her out too, if he gets the chance.

My gaze falls on the tray of food on the floor. I might as well eat to keep up my strength. I pick up a peanut butter sandwich and study it. Gary could have put something in it. I reach for the bottle of water next to the plate and eye it suspiciously from all angles. I can't tell if it's been tampered with, but I can't risk finding out. I toss the sandwich back on the plate, then shove the tray to one side. The plate slides across it revealing a folded slip of paper. I snatch it up and begin reading.

We're leaving tonight. You have to get out. He held a gun with a silencer to my head and said it was for you.

CHAPTER 42

The hours drag by, and I lose track of time. It's dark outside with only a trickle of moonlight lighting up the sky. I'm becoming increasingly erratic in my thoughts — on the verge of breaking down and hammering on the door, begging to be let out, or trying to smash the glass in the window and jumping. But I'd be leaping to certain death from this height in the dark. It's not as if I'm some kind of gifted free climber and could shimmy down the siding. I have a better chance of survival if I wait it out here and focus on keeping my wits about me.

I haven't heard anyone moving around in the house in a while. Nor have I heard a car engine starting up. I can't tell if Gary and Luna are still here, or if they've already left. Luna made it sound as though Gary was going to finish me off first, but maybe he changed his mind. Or perhaps she managed to talk him out of it. I can't help wondering why he's taking Luna with him. As some kind of insurance policy? It's possible he needs her signature to get his hands on Beth's inheritance. Whatever the reason, it's clear he has no use for me.

Just when I've convinced myself that Gary has left me alone to starve to death in this room, I hear footsteps approaching. My heart thuds in my chest. I throw myself back down on the floor and drape the severed rope strategically over my ankles, then place my hands behind my back. The door swings open and Gary strides in. "It's time," he says cryptically, walking over to the window. He checks to make sure I haven't placed anything on the glass or stashed a sign behind the curtains.

To my relief, I don't spot a gun bulging beneath his shirt. It's now or never. Whatever his intentions are for me, they can't be good. Silently, I get to my feet and spring at him, stabbing the knife into his gut. He groans and crumples over, clutching his side. I turn and dash out of the room, slamming the door shut behind me. To my horror, the key isn't in the lock. For a split second, I hesitate, wondering if I should search for Luna or run for help. My feet make the decision for me and, before I realize what's happening, I'm thundering down the stairs and out the back door. Tears of relief and terror stream down my face as I bolt across the lawn. In my mad sprint for freedom, I become aware that I'm still holding the bloody knife in my hand. Making a spur-of-the-moment decision, I run to the bottom of the garden and fling it as hard as I can over the fence into the wooded area beyond.

Bursting through the back door into the kitchen, I come to a screeching halt at the astonishing sight of Warren standing in front of the fridge holding a glass of water. Blood drains from my head and the room begins to spin around me.

"You're alive!" I gasp.

"Kay! Where have you been all this time?" he stammers, setting down his glass.

I run into his arms sobbing. "Gary was holding me prisoner. He was threatening to kill me."

"What are you talking about? I got your text that you were going out for drinks with Amber, but I was getting worried — I didn't expect you to get back so late."

I shake my head. "That wasn't me. Gary must have sent that text from my phone." I bury my face in his chest. "He told me you were dead."

Warren rubs a hand over my head gently. "Of course I'm not dead. What on earth are you talking about?"

"I . . . I think I might have killed him."

Warren grabs me by the shoulders and holds me away from him so he can look me in the eyes. "*What* did you say?"

"I was right about Gary all along," I blurt out through my tears. "I saw a sign in the window saying, 'Help me.' I went over there again and found Luna tied up to the bed. She says she thinks Gary killed her mother. I was trying to free her when he walked in on us. He tied me up to the bed as well and drugged me. I was out for hours." I swallow the lump in my throat. "He told me he'd killed you, but he was only goading me again. And now I've gone and killed him."

Warren draws in a hard breath. "How? Tell me exactly what happened."

"I stabbed him. Luna snuck a knife into the room when she brought me up a tray of food."

Warren frowns. "Was it a steak knife — serrated edge?"

"Yes. How did you know?"

"There's one missing from our knife block." He releases me and runs a hand through his hair, a perturbed look on his face.

"What are you saying?"

He lets out a weary sigh. "I don't think Luna was helping you, Kay. I think she was setting you up to do her dirty work for her."

155

CHAPTER 43

My mouth drops open. "What? No! You've got it all wrong. Gary beat Luna up. I saw her. Her face was black and blue. She told me he held a gun to her head and said it was for me. She snuck that knife into my room so I could escape. Maybe she was hoping I would stab him in the process, but she was trying to help me. She knew he was planning to kill me before they left tonight."

Warren squeezes my arm, his face contorted with horror. "Don't you realize what she's done? She took our knife, so it looks premeditated."

"That's ridiculous. How could she have got ahold of it when Gary was holding her prisoner?"

"The knife's been missing ever since she got here," Warren replies in a grim tone. "I meant to ask you about it, but I kept forgetting. It's possible she was planning to kill him all along and pin the blame on one of us. Where is the knife now?"

I shake my head. "I don't know. I tossed it over the fence at the bottom of the garden. It's somewhere in the woods."

Warren grimaces. "I'll grab a flashlight and see if I can find it." He disappears out the back door and darts down to the garden shed before I can talk him out of it.

I sink down in a kitchen chair, trembling all over. I'm pretty sure Warren shouldn't be handling the knife, even if he manages to find it in the pitch black of night. Isn't that technically contaminating evidence? I need to call the police, but I don't have my phone on me.

A shiver ripples over my shoulders. What if Gary comes crashing through the door? I'm not sure how badly injured he is, or if he's even capable of pursuing me, but I don't trust him as long as there's breath in his lungs. And Luna's still trapped in the house. She's depending on me coming to her rescue. I don't care what Warren says — I know her intention was to help me. Maybe she took the knife for protection that first night when I filled her head with my suspicions about what Gary did to her mother.

I can't sit here waiting for Warren to return. I need to call the police now. If Warren's phone isn't around here somewhere, I'll ring every doorbell on the street until someone answers. I get to my feet and walk over to the desk area in the corner of the kitchen. To my relief, Warren's phone is charging on the shelf above. I dial 911 and stumble through an abbreviated account of what happened. When I hang up, I'm tempted to call Officer Engelmann just for the satisfaction of letting him know I was right about my neighbor after all. But I don't have the energy to go over everything again. He'll hear about it soon enough.

Warren returns a short time later with a grave look on his face.

"Did you find the knife?" I ask.

He shakes his head. "No. It's too dark out there. But I went next door to check on Gary. He's dead. Looks like he bled out. We need to call the police."

"I already did. They're on their way." I press my trembling hands to my cheeks. "I can't believe he's really dead. I didn't mean to kill him. I was just trying to fight my way out of there. What about Luna, did you find her?"

"She's not in the house. I checked in all the rooms and yelled for her. She must have fled."

"I don't know how she could have escaped. Gary might have killed her before he came to get me. He could have put her body in the trunk of his car to dispose of later."

We both look up at the sound of sirens. Warren grabs me by the arms and looks intently into my eyes. "Listen to me, Kay. You can't tell the cops where that knife is. If they find it, it's going to look as if this whole thing was premeditated. You're going to have a tough time convincing them otherwise when Luna's not here to back up your story."

"It's not a story. It's the truth. They can check the bedroom where Gary tied me up. I left the cut zip ties on the floor, and the tray with the food. You must have seen it."

Warren frowns. "There was nothing there. The room was undisturbed, just like last time. The other bedrooms too."

I'm about to respond when the emergency vehicles screech to a halt outside. My heart slugs against my chest. Gary couldn't have cleaned the room up. He's dead. That leaves only one other person who could have gotten rid of the evidence.

CHAPTER 44

I'm barely functioning by the time the police knock on our door. Warren has convinced me there's a strong possibility they will bring charges against me if I tell them where the knife is, and it turns out to be ours. Against my better judgement, I've agreed to lie and tell them I left it in Gary's body. It will be up to them to figure out what happened to it. I can't pretend I didn't stab him, but I can claim self-defense. I don't know what to make of the fact that all the evidence of my imprisonment has disappeared from the room. Could Luna have gotten rid of the zip ties and food? Or did Gary dispose of it before he succumbed to his injuries?

Warren opens the door to Officer Engelmann, who is accompanied by a bug-eyed plainclothes detective.

"I'm sorry to hear about your ordeal Mrs. Mellows," Engelmann begins. "This is my colleague, Detective Slater."

"Call me Kay, please," I say. "Is he . . . is Gary dead?"

"Yes, ma'am," Slater replies. "We've conducted an initial investigation of the crime scene. Can you tell us exactly what happened in your own words?"

I take a deep breath and relay the gist of it again in a somewhat disjointed fashion. "Parts of it are still a blur. Gary tied me up and threatened to kill me. At one point, he gave me something to drink. He must have put a sedative in it because I was out for several hours. When Luna brought me something to eat, she warned me that he had a gun with a silencer, and that he was threatening to kill me. He had beaten her up pretty badly — I never saw her again after she brought me that tray of food. I think he might have killed her. I . . . I had no choice but to stab him to get away. I'm afraid he might have killed his wife, Beth, too."

Detective Slater hefts an eyebrow. "What makes you say that?"

"When Beth disappeared, he told everybody she'd checked herself into a rehab facility. But, according to her daughter, she wasn't an addict. She did seem a bit out of it at times, but I think Gary was drugging her. We had him over for dinner a few weeks after Beth disappeared, and he told us she'd passed away. He claimed he'd been too distraught to tell anyone about it, and he wasn't allowed to discuss the case anyway, because he was suing the facility. I didn't buy his story. I was already concerned for Beth's safety when she was living next door. Gary never would give me the name of the facility she supposedly checked into. He was very evasive any time I asked him about it."

"We'll look into it," Officer Engelmann says, tapping on his phone. It doesn't give me much reassurance, coming from him. I'm pretty sure he's already dismissed my concerns, even though Luna has disappeared now too. Maybe Detective Slater will take it more seriously.

"Getting back to the moment you escaped," Slater goes on, "can you show me exactly where you stabbed Gary?"

"Right around here," I say, pointing to my left side. "More toward the back. He was facing away from me."

Slater jots down the information. "How many times did you stab him?"

"Just once. I fled the minute he doubled over."

Slater and Engelmann exchange a loaded look.

I pucker my brow and turn to Warren to see if he's picked up on their odd reaction, but he's staring at his phone with a distracted look on his face.

Slater clears his throat to get my attention. "Can you describe the knife that Luna gave you when she brought your food?"

My stomach twists. I pride myself on being an honest person. The very idea of lying to the police is giving me hot flashes. "Um . . . I didn't look at it very closely. I was in complete panic mode."

"Understandable," Slater responds, with a sympathetic nod. "Did you happen to notice if the blade was serrated?"

"Yes, I believe so." I'm unable to hold his gaze. He's got to know I'm hiding something.

He glances over at the knife block in full view on our kitchen counter. I close my eyes briefly. I should have known he'd spot it.

"Looks like you're missing one of your knives." Slater looks between me and Warren, inviting either one of us to answer.

"Really?" Warren responds, blinking as though he's only just noticed it. "It's probably in the dishwasher."

Officer Engelmann gets to his feet and walks over to it. He opens the door and peers inside. "Nothing. It's empty."

I twist the button on the sleeve of my blouse until it's tight enough to pop off. My throat feels like dehydrated hide. I'm sweating profusely, and deeply regret agreeing to lie about the knife. I realize Warren only came up with that plan to protect me, but I've done nothing wrong. Surely the police would have come to the same conclusion themselves, if I'd let things play out. Now they're probably going to search the property, and they'll assume I'm guilty when they find my missing kitchen knife.

"The thing is, Kay," Slater goes on, his tone more honeyed than before, "we weren't able to find any evidence of your imprisonment in Gary's house. The guest bedroom was immaculate when we searched it. No remnants of zip ties or rope lying on the carpet or in the trash can. No tray of food. We didn't find any evidence that Luna had been locked in a bathroom, either."

I wet my lips, looking in desperation between Engelmann and Slater, and not finding a soft landing in either of their expressions. I have a sinking feeling I know how this will go down. I complained to several people in the neighborhood about my renter. They knew I didn't trust him and wanted him out. I even spread rumors about him doing away with his wife.

Ironically, I'm going to be the one on trial for murder.

CHAPTER 45

"It all feels so surreal," I say to Amber the following day. "I woke up thinking it was just a bad dream for about two seconds before it hit me all over again."

I've just finished recounting everything that happened, and Amber looks as shell-shocked as I feel inside.

"I think you should tell the police the truth about what you did with the knife," she says. "They always find out in the end when someone's lying, and it only makes you look more guilty."

I wring my hands in my lap. "But they'll arrest me if they find out the knife came from my house. How am I supposed to explain that? They'll think I took it with me when I went to confront Gary, which makes it premeditated murder and not self-defense." I drop my head into my hands and groan. "I'm the president of the HOA. How is this happening to me?"

Amber arches a brow. "What's that got to do with anything?"

I stare at her in disbelief. "I'm supposed to be the one who reports crime in the neighborhood. Now I'm going to be splattered across the tabloids in one unflattering headline after another."

"You're getting ahead of yourself," Amber replies. "You need to calm down and think things through. Even if the knife came from your kitchen, it's a clear case of self-defense."

"How do you figure?" I throw up my hands in frustration. "There's no evidence to support what I told the police."

"Luna will verify everything you've said once they find her."

I cringe at the mention of her name. I dread to think what might have befallen her at Gary's hands. Warren has been casting aspersions on her, but I saw her injuries and distress firsthand. "She's vanished without a trace," I say. "I'd like to believe she escaped, but that's wishful thinking on my part. I'm pretty sure Gary killed her. The police might never find her body."

Amber rolls her eyes. "And once again, you're jumping to conclusions. You don't even know that she's dead."

I rub my hands over my face. "The last time I saw her she was pretty close to death's door. I've never seen someone so badly beaten. Do you really think he would let her live after doing that to her?"

"Well, I'll do what I can to help you prove your case. I can at least vouch for the fact that Beth was an abused woman. I saw how Gary controlled her."

I give her a watery smile. "Thanks Amber. It helps to know you've got my back."

My phone rings and I grimace when I see the name on the screen. "It's Officer Engelmann."

Amber's eyes widen. "Maybe they've found Luna."

"Alive, hopefully," I say, as I take the call.

"Good morning, Kay," Engelmann begins. "We'd like you to come down to the station so we can take your official statement."

My pulse thunders in my ears. "'Official' — what does that mean? Do I need a lawyer?"

"That's entirely up to you. We just need you to go over what you told us yesterday and sign a written statement. It won't take long."

"I can probably be there within the hour."

I hang up and gawk at Amber. "What should I do? If I show up with a lawyer in tow, it's going to look like I have something to hide."

"Just read your statement through and sign it. If they start to question you again, ask for a lawyer. Don't overthink it. I'm sure it's just a standard step in the process. I'll drive you, if you want."

Despite Amber's reassurances, I'm not convinced it's going to be as straightforward as she thinks. I call Warren at work to update him, only to discover that he's been summoned too.

"Should I wait for you so we can go in together?" I ask. It will be a lot less intimidating to have Warren by my side.

"No point. They want to interview us separately," he replies.

"I didn't realize it was an interview. I thought they just wanted me to sign a written statement — at least that's what they told me."

There's a long pause before Warren responds. "You can't trust the police. If they suspect foul play on our part, they're not going to inform us of their suspicions."

The knot in the pit of my stomach tightens. "So, do we need representation or not?"

"If they tell you you're a person of interest, lawyer up. If they just ask you to recap what you told them at the house and sign it, you're good."

Amber drives me to the police station, and I head inside on shaky legs, only partly reassured by Warren's explanation. Detective Slater escorts me into an interview room where Officer Engelmann is already seated next to a recording device. I'm parched, but I'm not sure if it's appropriate to ask for something to drink. Aren't they supposed to offer me water, at the very least? Detective Slater jumps right in, assuring me that I'm here on my own volition and can leave whenever I want to. I nod but squirm, feeling like a criminal under his keen gaze.

"I'm going to go over the same questions I asked you yesterday," he says. "Take as much time as you need to answer, and afterward I'll have you sign your statement."

I blink back at him, acid swirling up my throat as I wait for him to begin. Engelmann switches on the recording device and notes the date and those present. I slowly begin to relax as Detective Slater leads me through the same series of questions I already went over at the house. I stick to the script, omitting the fact that I disposed of the bloody knife in the woods at the bottom of the garden.

Just when I think we've reached the end of the interview, Slater throws me for a loop.

"I'm happy to report that we've located Gary's step-daughter, Luna Webster."

CHAPTER 46

"Is she . . . alive?" I ask, mentally bracing myself for the worst. Slater's expression gives nothing away.

"Yes, she's alive," he replies, tapping the end of his pen on the desk.

I press a hand to my chest, relief flooding through me. "That's wonderful news. I was scared Gary might have killed her. Is she badly injured?"

Detective Slater rubs a hand over his jaw. "She's fine."

I frown, thrown off by his casual tone. "Is she at the hospital? Her face was badly beaten. I'm worried her cheek might be fractured."

"You needn't be concerned about her. She's being well taken care of."

I tug at a strand of hair, uncertain what that means. Luna could be in surgery, for all I know. But I guess that's all I'm going to get out of Slater, for now. He probably can't divulge any medical information due to privacy laws. At least Luna managed to escape from Gary's clutches. I would have felt awful if she'd died at his hands after I'd left her behind. "How did she get away?" I ask.

I glance over at Officer Engelmann, but he avoids looking directly at me. I've never felt like that man was on my side.

Slater runs a hand over his thinning hair. "Luna said she fled the house after you stabbed her stepfather."

A shiver runs across my shoulders. "I'm glad she managed to get free. If he'd gotten his hands on her, he might have finished her off."

Slater taps his fingers thoughtfully on the table in front of him. "To be precise, she said she fled the house after you *attacked* her stepfather."

My lips form a response, but nothing comes out of my mouth but a small squeak. I can't quite grasp the quantum leap from self-defense to assault. Is Slater trying to shock me into admitting to doing something I didn't? I've watched enough true crime shows to know that it's perfectly legal for the police to lie to you during an investigation. That must be what he's doing — testing me to see if I'll confess to murdering my neighbor. Anger flushes through my veins. How dare they accuse me of attacking Gary? I was trying to save my life, and Luna's. All I've ever done is look out for my neighbors, which is why I'm in this mess to begin with.

"I'm not sure what you're implying, but you're way off base," I snap. "Gary was holding me prisoner. I barely escaped with my life."

Slater doesn't miss a beat with his incessant tapping. "Luna maintains you've been interfering in her parents' lives since the day they moved in. Harassing them with unfounded accusations, spying on them through binoculars, and spreading rumors about them in the neighborhood. Any of that ring a bell?"

My cheeks flush. "It's my job as president of the HOA to keep an eye on things. I was only looking out for Beth Finkel's well-being. It was evident to me, and others, that she was being abused."

Slater leans back in his chair. "Who are the *others* you mentioned who can corroborate this?"

"My husband, for one. And Maria Torres, my neighbor. And Amber Demkovich. She's a friend and neighbor."

Slater reaches for a pen. "Spell that for me, would you?"

He jots it down and I take several deep breaths, my hands folded in my lap. I need to stay calm. I won't do myself any favors by acting like the crazy neighborhood watch lady who attacked Luna's stepfather. What on earth convinced her to say something like that, after everything Gary put her through? Isn't emotional attachment to an abuser a symptom of Stockholm syndrome? But she's out of his clutches now. It makes no sense.

I suddenly remember what Engelmann told me Luna said to him on the phone a few weeks back — something about me making her uncomfortable by insinuating that her step-dad was abusing her mother. When I asked her about it, she denied he had ever spoken to her, but what if she was lying? What if everything she told me was a lie? My heart sinks further as Warren's words come back to haunt me: *I don't think Luna was helping you, Kay. I think she was setting you up to do her dirty work for her.*

Did she set me up to kill Gary? I press my fingertips to my temples, suddenly unsure of what's real anymore. "You must have noticed that Luna's face was black and blue," I say. "Did she tell you Gary beat her?"

Slater presses his lips together in a tight line. "I understand that's what you thought you saw, but I can assure you that Luna is uninjured."

Heat prickles over my skin. Did I really see bruises on Luna's face? Or was I hallucinating again? "So, what are you saying? Do you think I'm making it up? Do you really think I murdered my neighbor?"

Slater gives a small smile, but there's nothing warm about it. "You've admitted to stabbing him."

"Yes!" I explode. "In self-defense!"

Slater sighs. "I want to believe you, Kay, but I know you're not telling me everything."

I sink back in my chair, deflating rapidly under his scrutiny. I can't keep lying to the police. What's the point in trying to conceal what I did with the knife? They'll search the area and find it eventually anyway. I'm almost at the point of confessing, but then I remember that I need to ask for a lawyer before I say anything that could incriminate me. I wonder if Warren has lawyered up already. "What do you want to know?" I ask, trying to stave off the inevitable.

Slater rests his elbows on the table in front of him and tents his fingers together. "You told us you stabbed Gary Finkel. The thing is, Kay, Gary didn't die from the injury to his side. He died from the stab wound to his chest."

CHAPTER 47

The hint of a smile plays on Slater's lips, but I'm not sure if he's exuding sympathy or trying to mask disdain. "Did you stab Gary more than once, Kay? It doesn't rule out the possibility that you acted in self-defense. But I need you to tell me the truth because something's not adding up."

"I . . . I did tell you the truth," I stammer, instantly second-guessing myself. *Did* I stab Gary more than once? My mind fogs with confusion. I try to replay the scene, but I'm becoming more disoriented by the minute. The room is oppressively hot and I'm finding it difficult to breathe. Maybe I'm having a panic attack.

"I want to believe you," Slater says.

I stare back at him, bug-eyed. I can't tell if he's being honest, or if he's just trying to build some level of trust so that I break down and tell him everything.

"There are discrepancies in your story, Kay. I need you to be honest with me, so we can get to the bottom of things," Slater goes on. "The coroner has completed his preliminary autopsy report. The knife that was used to inflict the chest wound wasn't the same one that was used to stab Gary in the side."

I mouth the words over again to myself, analyzing them. My head is spinning. "Are you saying I didn't kill Gary?"

"I'm saying that whoever stabbed him in the chest delivered the fatal wound," Slater replies in a wooden tone.

"But that means . . ." I trail off, trying to come to terms with the implications. "Luna must have stabbed him before she fled the scene."

Slater's expression remains impassive. "It's an angle we have to consider. She denies knowing anything about it."

I frown. Did she lie about me to save her own skin — because she was afraid of the consequences? "But it would still be considered self-defense, right, if she killed him?"

"It depends on the circumstances — whether she felt threatened or not."

"He threatened her with a gun."

"There's no evidence that Gary had a gun," Slater says. "We searched the house thoroughly. We haven't found the second knife either — the one that was used to deliver the fatal blow."

Slater holds my gaze for a long moment. "I need to ask you about the timeline after you escaped from Gary. Can you go over again what happened from the moment you arrived home until the moment the police knocked on your door?"

I frown, trying to recall the chain of events. "Everything's such a blur. I was dreading what I would find inside my house. I thought Gary had killed Warren — he insinuated as much. I couldn't believe it when I got home and saw my husband standing in the kitchen holding a glass of water. I thought I was hallucinating. He told me he'd gotten a message from my phone to say I was out with Amber. Gary must have sent that text so Warren wouldn't come looking for me." I pull out a tissue and dab at the tears springing to my eyes. It pains me to think how close I came to losing my husband.

"What was Warren's response when you told him what you'd done?" Slater asks.

"He was shocked, naturally. He wanted to know exactly what happened. And he asked me where the knife was."

Slater leans forward, his eyes glinting under the fluorescent light. "What did you tell him?"

I drop my gaze to my shaking fingers. "I . . . I tossed the knife over the fence into the woods at the bottom of our garden." I sniff back a sob. "I wasn't thinking straight. I saw the blood and wanted to get rid of it as quickly as possible. I wasn't trying to hide anything."

Slater turns to Engelmann. "Get someone on that right away."

Engelmann gets to his feet with a curt nod and exits the room.

"Is there anything else you want to tell me, Kay?" Slater asks in an innocuous monotone.

I shake my head. I'm not about to tell him that it was Warren's idea to lie about the knife. He was only trying to protect me.

"Do you think it was the missing knife from your block?" Slater asks.

"I honestly don't know. Like I said, I didn't look at it too closely. I suppose it could have been ours, but I didn't take it with me to Gary's house. I remember wishing that I'd brought the gun from our safe."

"I appreciate you coming clean with me," Slater says, switching off the recording device. "It's imperative that we find the knife you used. If your DNA is on it, and it matches the wound in Gary's side, it will prove you inflicted the first non-fatal wound."

The measure of relief I feel is overshadowed by a foreboding thought. If I didn't inflict the fatal wound, and Luna fled the scene after I stabbed Gary, there's only one other person who had the opportunity to kill him.

CHAPTER 48

After I sign my statement, Amber escorts me out to her car and I buckle myself into the passenger seat in a daze.

"Are you okay?" she asks, eyeing me warily.

I let out a weighty sigh. "I'm not sure. In fact, I'm not sure about anything right now."

"Why? What happened in there? You're not under arrest, so that's a good sign, right?"

"That could be about to change. I fessed up and told the cops I tossed the knife. They dispatched someone to retrieve it." I scratch distractedly at my neck. It feels like my skin is itching all over. I don't like the dark thoughts encircling my mind like an iron clamp, but I don't know how to make them go away. "The weird thing is that the detective who took my statement said Gary was stabbed twice," I say. "The second wound, the fatal one, was to his chest. Two different knives were used." I hesitate, studying Amber's expression to see if she's grasped the implications.

Her jaw drops. "Are you saying Luna killed him?"

"I don't know. It's possible. I'm afraid she might have set me up, or maybe . . ." I break off, not wanting to voice the terrifying thought that's been jittering around at the back of my mind ever since I learned that Gary was stabbed twice. There was one other person who entered the house after I escaped. I can't comprehend my mild-mannered husband stabbing our renter.

But then again, I managed to do it. Perhaps Gary lunged at Warren, and he was forced to defend himself. But where did he get the knife from? Did he take it with him? Wouldn't that be considered premeditation? And what did he do with the knife afterward? My head hurts from the sheer volume of questions swirling around inside. Why didn't Warren tell me what he'd done? I can understand why he was loath to confess to the police, but why hide it from me?

"Maybe what?" Amber prods.

I shake my head. "Nothing." I don't want to cast aspersions on Warren before I have a chance to talk with him. I'm hoping he won't be held up at the police station for much longer. "I'm just trying to figure out Luna's motivation for lying about me. She told Engelmann that I attacked her stepfather."

Amber's eyes grow wide. "Are you kidding me? After all you did for her? Why on earth would she say something like that?"

I shrug helplessly. "Fear, maybe? She seemed to be genuinely terrified of Gary."

"But she has no reason to be anymore. The man's dead. Why doesn't she come clean to the police now?"

"Maybe it's some kind of Stockholm syndrome thing she has to break free of."

Amber starts the engine. "So, where does that leave you?"

"Good question," I say, hugging my arms around myself. "Hunting for a lawyer, for starters. I'm pretty sure I'm a person of interest, even though the cops aren't coming right out and saying as much."

My phone rings as Amber pulls into our driveway ten minutes later. I fish it out of my purse and check to see who's calling. "It's that private investigator I hired to look into Gary," I say, putting the call on speaker.

"Hi, Kay. Sorry it's taken me so long to get back to you," George says. "I had a couple of emergency situations come up. Anyway, I do have some information for you on your renter. It should be enough to give you grounds to evict him, if nothing else."

I scrunch my eyes shut. "Too late for that, I'm afraid. He's dead."

George is silent for a moment before responding. "Mind if I ask what happened?"

I freeze, unable to force myself to utter the words: *I stabbed him.*

"Hey, George!" Amber cuts in. "This is Kay's friend, Amber. Kay's pretty cut up about the whole thing. It's hard for her to talk about it, to be honest. It's kind of a long story, but we believe he was stabbed to death by his stepdaughter."

George lets out a long, low whistle. "What goes around comes around, I guess."

"What do you mean?" I ask, finally finding my voice.

"It took a bit of digging, but I managed to get the scoop on your mystery man next door. Gary Finkel's not his real name. He's had more than one alias over the years, but he goes by Larry Davis on his birth certificate."

My heart is racing so fast I feel like I might be sick. I'm waiting for George to tell me what I've suspected all along: that Gary — Larry — is a criminal. A conman. A serial killer. A kidnapper. A psychopath. All of the above, and then some. Who knows how many other crimes he might have notched on his belt over the years? Why else would someone use aliases if not to hide their illegal activities?

"Did you find out anything else about him?" I ask.

"Yes. This is where it gets interesting. He's not actually married to Beth Finkel — her real name is Elizabeth Lee. As far as I can tell, they've been together ever since his first wife died. Apparently, she drowned in the bathtub after overdosing. And before you ask, it was ruled an accidental death. I'll send you over all the information I have on it."

My scalp prickles. Alarm bells are going off in my head in quick succession. If Gary killed Beth, what's to say he didn't kill his wife too? It may have been ruled an accident at the time, but Slater might be willing to take another look at it now that Beth has gone missing.

I thank George and hang up after promising to mail him a check for his services to date.

Amber accompanies me into the house and brews us both a strong cup of tea. "I guess you were right about your next-door neighbor after all," she says, sinking onto the couch next to me. "You had a bad feeling about him from the very beginning."

I give a mute nod as I raise the cup to my lips. The problem is, he's not the only person I have a bad feeling about.

CHAPTER 49

Amber makes me a sandwich but I have no appetite, and I pick at it listlessly as we wait for Warren to return. As the minutes tick by, I become increasingly anxious, my suspicions compounding. Why is it taking him so long to give a statement? He only discovered the body — at least, that's what he led me to believe. But the more I think about it, the more it makes sense that Warren might have been the one who delivered the fatal blow. He would hardly have been foolish enough to go next door without some kind of weapon in hand, especially after finding out that Gary had imprisoned me and Luna and threatened us with bodily harm — even going so far as to hold a gun to Luna's head.

Warren might have stopped by the garden shed and grabbed a knife from his toolbox as a precautionary measure. I frown as I sip my tea. But wouldn't he have been covered with blood if he had stabbed Gary in the chest? I'm picturing that as a much messier scenario than stabbing someone from behind, but what do I know about blood splatter and crime scenes?

"I can stay with you until Warren gets back, if you like," Amber offers, glancing at her watch.

I give her a grateful smile. "I appreciate it, but there's really no need. You should go home. I have no idea how much longer he's going to be."

The truth is, I'm ready for Amber to leave. I want to do some investigating, but I don't want to tip her off as to what I'm up to. I'm hoping I'm wrong about my suspicions, and I don't want her thinking badly of Warren unnecessarily. Or worse, spreading rumors about him around the neighborhood. Ironic, I know, considering I did the same thing to Gary — or Larry, as it turns out. But in my case, it was justified.

Amber drains her cup and gets to her feet. "If you're sure you'll be okay, I'll head home and get some work done. Text me when Warren gets back, so I don't worry about you sitting here alone all evening."

I accompany her to the door and hug her tightly. "Thanks, Amber. I don't know how I would get through this without you. I just wish I could have done more for Beth."

"You were the best friend and neighbor you could have been under the circumstances," she assures me. "It's not your fault the police didn't take your concerns seriously. Don't beat yourself up about it. At least Gary can't hurt anyone else now."

The minute Amber drives off, I hurry down to the garden shed and push open the door. As fastidious as Warren is about his tools, I'm certain I'll be able to spot if anything's missing. He built one of those custom tool organization boards, so he has a specific place for every one of his tools. At first glance, I can't see anything missing. I walk over to his wheeled workbench and pull out the top drawer. An array of gleaming socket wrenches and screwdrivers are lined up inside, from smallest to largest. I go through the rest of the drawers and find all the tools arrayed in a similar manner. Nothing is out of place.

Next, I turn my attention to the tool bag sitting on a stool in the corner and begin rummaging aimlessly through it. My heart skips a beat when I come across an empty leather sheath in one of the side pockets. I recognize it right away. It belongs to the hunting knife I bought Warren last Christmas. I swallow the knot of panic surging up my throat as I cast a desperate glance around the shed, hoping in vain to spot the knife somewhere. But Warren never leaves his tools lying around. The minute he's done with something, he returns it to its designated spot.

There can be only one reason why the knife is missing.

CHAPTER 50

I hurry back up to the house, breathing in ragged spurts as I struggle to come to terms with what I've discovered. Could there be another explanation for the missing hunting knife? Maybe Luna stole it. I try texting Warren to ask him about it, but he doesn't answer. If the police are still interviewing him, he's hardly in a position to check his messages. I have no choice but to wait on tenterhooks until he calls me back.

I pace across the kitchen floor, hands tucked into my armpits, trying to figure out what all this means for our relationship. It's not the fact that Warren might have stabbed Gary to death that's tearing me apart — truth be told, I'm glad he's dead — it's the fact that Warren concealed it from me, and worse, he let me take the blame. I'm suddenly questioning everything. I can't help wondering if there's anything else he's hiding from me. Did he know Gary's real name was Larry Davis? Am I crazy for thinking this way? Doesn't it make more sense to believe Luna killed Gary? Was he even her stepfather? I move into the hall and eye the door to Warren's office with a trepidatious feeling in my gut. I've never snooped around in there before, but my investigative radar is drawing me to that room.

I get to work going through the drawers in Warren's desk, all of which are as meticulously organized as his tool shed. I'm only too aware that he could return at any minute, so I'm making the most of the opportunity by working efficiently, while making sure to put everything back the way I found it. I don't even know what I'm looking for, but I hope I don't stumble on the murder weapon. I'm not about to hide another bloody knife from the police, no matter the consequences.

I shuffle through a stack of papers in a wire tray on the desk and discover a notepad lodged beneath. Holding it up to the light, I squint at it, trying to make out the imprint of the last thing Warren wrote, but I can't decipher anything. I carefully arrange everything back into a neat pile, then turn on Warren's computer. I enter the password, relieved to see he hasn't changed it — which would definitely have been an indication of guilt. He probably doesn't think I know his password, but I've surreptitiously watched him enter it over his shoulder — just in case I ever needed to access his computer in an emergency, like now.

It slowly powers up, and I begin scrolling through Warren's unanswered emails, feeling increasingly like a creep for doubting him. I feel perfectly justified keeping a close watch on my neighbors, but spying on my own husband is another thing entirely. I don't particularly need to know that he ordered a tube of hemorrhoid cream on Amazon, or that his boss is less than impressed with the numbers on his latest sales presentation.

After several more minutes of fruitless scrolling, I abandon the emails and move on to Warren's browser. I scan through the history, but it's mostly YouTube videos — everything from organizational tips, to hunting, to rebuilding motorcycles. I click on an unusual-looking link that leads to the product page of some kind of overseas marketplace website.

The breath leaves my lungs when I see what Warren has ordered.

CHAPTER 51

My eyes race across the screen reading the names of the drugs displayed on the website. *Dexanol, quetfluramine, seroquitin, zopiclonin* — on and on it goes. I move my cursor over to the shopping cart icon and click on the previous orders tab. *Psilocinone.* What is this stuff? I drill down on the product page and read the description. I'm still not sure exactly what it is I'm looking at, so I copy and paste the name of the prescription into Google and do a search for side effects. A strange tingling sensation goes through me as I begin to read.

> *Can induce acute changes in the perception of self, time, and space. May produce powerful alterations of mood and vivid visual hallucinations. Might cause—*

The sound of the garage door opening startles me almost out of my skin. Warren's car pulls in and the engine turns off, triggering my flight or fight response. I switch off the computer, leap to my feet, and dash out of the office.

"Hey," he says, tossing his keys on the kitchen table as he strides in. He ruffles his hair and yawns loudly. "Can you believe the cops kept me there for almost four hours? What time did you get back?"

"A couple of hours ago." I fidget with the hem of my sweater. "What did they ask you about?"

He scrubs a hand over his face, avoiding my gaze. "Same old stuff they went over already. I think they just wanted to make sure we had our stories straight." He walks over to me and lays his hands on my shoulders, gazing intently at me. "And we do, don't we? You didn't tell them about the knife, did you?"

I flinch at the word. I can almost feel the steel blade piercing my belly. I can barely keep myself from trembling. Only this time it's not Gary I'm afraid of. I wonder how my ordinarily mild-mannered husband would react if I told him I suspected him of killing Gary and drugging me. "Of course not," I lie.

"You're shaking," Warren says, rubbing my arms briskly. "Are you cold?"

"A little."

"You need to eat something, we both do after the grilling we got," he says firmly. "Go sit down. I'll fix us a sandwich."

I let out a silent sigh of relief as I retire to the family room and turn on the gas fire. I need a minute to compose myself. It's too hard to keep pretending everything's all right between us when I know what Warren's hiding from me. I need to have it out with him, sooner rather than later. All I want to do is grab him and shake the truth out of him — demand that he tells me where his hunting knife is, and why he's secretly been dosing me with hallucinogens. Because what other explanation is there? He kept trying to convince me to write off the strange nightmares I've been having of late as stress-related, but I've never reacted to stress like this before. I suspected Gary was drugging Beth, but it never occurred to me that my own husband was drugging me too. Did I give him the idea by sharing my suspicions about Gary? But why did he do it? What could he possibly have to gain by making me look like I was loopy? Was he planning on making me disappear like Gary made Beth disappear?

"Here you go, honey," Warren says, walking in with a tray of sandwiches and two glasses of iced tea.

My eyes bulge when it suddenly occurs to me that he might have doctored my drink. He sets the glass down on a coaster on the end table next to me and hands me a plate.

"Roast beef and pepper jack — your favorite." He grins at me as he sinks down on the couch and dives straight into his sandwich. I take a small bite and chew woodenly. I have no appetite, and it takes several attempts before I manage to swallow the congealed ball of bread and meat stuck in my throat. There's no way I'm touching that iced tea, but I desperately need something to drink. I set my plate to one side and get to my feet. "I think I'll grab a water. I'm really dehydrated after talking to the cops for two hours straight."

I retreat to the kitchen and pour myself a glass, downing it in one go before refilling it. My brain is abuzz with discordant theories. Maybe I've got this all wrong, and Warren was buying the drugs for Gary. Did he do it under duress? Was Gary holding something over his head? Is that why Warren finished him off when I told him I'd stabbed him? Either way, I need to proceed with caution before I confront my husband with what I found on his computer. If it turns out that he's been drugging me and gaslighting me about everything, I might be in real danger. I'll wait until he's asleep and then do some more snooping around.

And this time, I'll leave no stone unturned.

CHAPTER 52

"Do you want to watch a movie?" Warren asks, after he finishes his sandwich. "I'm too jacked up to sleep after that interrogation."

I stare at him aghast. "How can you focus on a movie right now? Our neighbor is dead. We've just been interviewed as persons of interest. What we should be doing is getting on the web and researching defense attorneys."

Warren lets out a long, shuddering sigh as he sinks back against the cushions. "I just don't want to think about it right now."

"Well, we don't have that luxury. We could end up fighting for our freedom if the cops decide to bring a murder case against us."

"We?" Warren blinks, a befuddled expression on his face. "They only interviewed me to make sure I wasn't covering for you. I'm not at risk of being charged with anything. You have nothing to worry about either; I told them you acted in self-defense. And you didn't kill Gary, Luna did."

I search his expression, wanting to believe him, but unable to quell the uneasy feeling sloshing back and forth in my gut. If I hadn't discovered the drug order on his computer, I might be able to convince myself that Luna took the knife from our shed with the intention of killing her stepfather. But the more I think about the symptoms I've been experiencing over the past few weeks, the less convinced I am that I can trust my husband.

We end up spending the next forty-five minutes research- ing legal representation and whittling it down to two choices, before Warren tosses his phone aside and gets to his feet. "Okay, that's enough for one night. Let's go to bed. We can make a decision in the morning."

I'm more wide awake than ever, but I pretend to yawn and follow him up to the bedroom. Adrenaline is pumping through my body, and I can hear my heart thudding in my chest. My hand shakes so badly while I'm cleaning my teeth that I drop my toothbrush into the sink twice. Thankfully, Warren's too busy with his nightly flossing routine to notice. Like everything else, he's very particular about his teeth.

It seems to take an eternity before he begins to snore lightly. I wait until I'm sure he's in a deep sleep, then gently turn back the duvet and slide my feet to the carpet. I tip- toe across the floor and pull the bedroom door closed behind me, before padding down the stairs to Warren's office. Safely inside, I take a quick calming breath before seating myself in front of the computer to finish what I started. I do a quick search for lawyers in the area and open up a couple of tabs just in case Warren walks in on me. I'll tell him I couldn't sleep and decided to do some more research.

I trawl through the rest of his browser history, but I don't find anything else incriminating. I bring up the overseas drug shopping website again and verify the date of the order. It was placed four days ago, which means it hasn't even been delivered yet. I frown at the screen and check the order his- tory again, but there's no record of any previous orders. Is it possible he bought the same drugs in the past from a different website? But why would it not show up in his history? Did he use his work laptop?

I can't believe I'm thinking this way about my husband. He's never been the devious sort. It drives him bonkers when

I get my binoculars out and start surveilling people on our street. And yet, here I am discovering uncomfortable secrets about him. I root around in the perfectly organized drawers in his desk again, taking care not to slam them shut for fear he might hear me.

My gaze lands on the trash can beneath the desk. I pick it up and poke around in the contents. It's mostly receipts, marketing mailers, and miscellaneous notes. I fish out a crumpled piece of paper and glance through the bullet points for a work meeting that's already come and gone. I toss it back into the trash can, then rummage around and pull out another discarded scrap of paper. Unfurling it, I read the words with a gnawing sense of disbelief and horror.

Beth Finkel's a thief.

CHAPTER 53

The cylinders in my head are misfiring, ricocheting random thoughts in myriad directions. It's the middle of the night and my brain feels like it's turning to mush. *Beth Finkel's a thief.* I'm trying to remember where I've heard that before. I'm fighting exhaustion, and overload, and a horrible feeling of foreboding that the person I trusted most in the whole world has betrayed me. The worst part about it is that I still don't know why. Did Warren and Gary make some kind of pact to get rid of their wives — starting with Beth? Luna showing up on the scene must have disrupted their plans. But how was Gary able to get her to lie about me after everything he did to her?

I shake my head free of my disturbing thoughts and turn my attention back to the note on the desk in front of me. And then it hits me. Maria found one just like it in her mailbox. She didn't recognize the handwriting, and I didn't think to ask if I could take a look at it. I wonder if she still has the note. It's too late to call her now, but I can try first thing in the morning. As shocking as it is to admit it, all the evidence points to Warren somehow being involved in helping Gary frame Beth — maybe even dispose of her. A cold shiver runs up my spine. I know my husband. He couldn't be induced to do something so horrendous unless he had no choice in the matter. Gary must have something big on him — but what?

I power down the computer and get to my feet. There's got to be more that Warren is hiding from me. I need to take a look at his phone and figure out if he's been communicating with Gary — or a Larry Davis — all along. If Warren catches me going through his phone, it will be a whole lot harder to explain myself, but I can't stop now. I need to know what he's been up to behind my back.

I turn off the light and step into the hallway, pulling the door closed behind me. A dark shape moves toward me, and I let out a blood-curdling scream.

"It's okay! It's only me!" Warren calls out. "What are you doing up?"

I press a hand to my chest. "You scared me half to death. I just came downstairs to get some water and I noticed the light was on in your office."

Warren frowns. "That's weird. I wasn't in there this evening."

"It was me," I say nonchalantly. "I was dusting earlier. I had to get my mind off things while I was waiting for you to get back from the station."

Warren tugs a hand through his tousled hair. "Go back to bed. I'll bring you up a glass of water."

I clutch the handrail for support as I mount the stairs, each step more leaden than the last. I don't know if he believed my spur-of-the-moment excuse. And I'm not sure if he's going to bring me up a glass of water or a kitchen knife.

CHAPTER 54

Apparently, I'm not going to die tonight after all. I reach for the glass of water Warren hands me, but my fingers are shaking too much to hold it.

"I'll set it on your bedside table," he says. "You should really try to get some rest, Kay. Your sleep patterns have been all over the place lately."

And now I know why. I lay my head back down on the pillow and close my eyes, willing myself to fall asleep, but I'm wide awake and more confused than ever. I can't figure out why Warren wrote that note. Did Gary order him to do it? Surely Warren didn't steal Maria Torres's purse from her house to frame Beth. Then again, if Gary has something substantial on him, Warren might have felt he had no choice but to do his bidding — even going so far as to drug me to stop me from meddling in the situation.

Before long, Warren is snoring again. I'm fearful he might be faking it, so I prod him gently in the side, but he doesn't react. Slowly, I repeat the process of exiting the bed without disturbing him. I take the glass of water with me. If he comes downstairs again, I'll pretend to be refilling it.

Filtered moonlight is spilling into the kitchen, bathing the counters in eerie shadows. My eyes go straight to the knife block on the counter. There's still only one knife missing, which is somewhat reassuring. At least Warren isn't sleeping with a blade under our mattress.

I walk over to the charging station where our phones lie side-by-side on the granite counter. After reading an article about the dangers of blue light interrupting sleep cycles, we made a pact a while back to stop taking our phones to bed with us. I grimace at my own naivety. It only helps you sleep better if your husband's not dosing you with psychedelics at the same time.

I reach for Warren's phone and unlock it with my finger. I added my fingerprint to the touch ID in the settings while he was watching a movie one night — not that I thought I'd ever need to use it to snoop on my husband. I just figured it would be a good idea in case there was ever an emergency, and I needed to access his phone. My vigilance is paying off now.

I sit for a moment in the shadows listening to the silence of our house at night. I can almost imagine I hear a creak on the floorboards upstairs, but as the minutes go by, no one appears in the doorway. Turning my attention back to Warren's phone, I open up the messages app and skim through the texts searching for Gary Finkel or Larry Davis. I scroll all the way to the bottom but find nothing. I know Warren communicated with him via text about the rental agreement. He must have deleted those messages.

I begin scrolling slowly back up through the texts, checking the odd one here and there — it's mostly work stuff, mutual friends, his mother, a car mechanic. I frown when I come to a name I don't recognize. *Checkers*. I scratch my forehead, trying in vain to dredge up a face to match it. What kind of a name is Checkers? I tap on the message and read it. *4517 West Acacia Blvd.* Presumably, Checkers lives at this address, but who is this person and why are they texting my husband?

There are no previous messages in the thread. Or if there were, they've been deleted too. My head is spinning. I'm only growing more perplexed with every new discovery. Could this be an address for an off-site client meeting?

Much as I'd like to believe it's work-related, that doesn't ring true. It's too abrupt — more like the kind of clandestine message a drug dealer would send a customer. Were drugs and money set to exchange hands at this location? I groan softly at the unwelcome thought. That explains why there were no previous orders on the overseas pharmaceutical website on Warren's computer.

His dealer is here in town.

CHAPTER 55

Somehow, I manage to make it through the rest of the night staring up at the ceiling and plotting my next moves. Warren takes off for work at 7.30 a.m. after making me promise to make an appointment with one of the two lawyers we've narrowed it down to. I have every intention of doing just that, but it's not my first priority this morning. I'm going to drive to West Acacia Boulevard and find out if my suspicions about Checkers' identity are correct. I thought drug dealers favored more ominous-sounding names, but maybe they're trending in a more benign direction nowadays. This isn't my area of expertise.

I dress casually and leave all my jewelry behind. I have no desire to look like an attractive target to every petty criminal working the street. After going back and forth on the issue, I open the safe and remove the gun. I'm not foolish enough to confront this Checkers individual unarmed. I never thought I could put a knife in Gary, but I surprised myself. I'd like to think if I'm about to become the victim of another crime, I could pull the trigger too. Let's hope I don't have to put that theory to the test.

I pull a beanie over my head and practice sulking in the mirror, so I look more streetwise than artlessly suburban. I'll probably stick out like a sore thumb in my Lexus — maybe I can park a few streets over from Acacia and walk the rest of the way. Taking an Uber is an option, but I don't want to be hanging around waiting on someone to pick me up afterward, especially if there are seedy characters with eyes on me. If things don't go well with this unidentified Checkers character, I might need to make a quick getaway.

I plonk my travel mug into the cupholder and plug the address into my GPS. I have about a forty-minute drive ahead of me. Plenty of time to back out if I change my mind. My heart is already thumping erratically as I pull out onto the street. I can't imagine how fast it will begin to beat when I come face to face with Checkers. I haven't settled on what I'm going to say to this person. They might not be willing to give me information on one of their customers, but maybe I don't need them to confirm anything. Once I mention Warren's name, one look will tell me all I need to know. The real question I want answered is why my husband was drugging me in the first place. There's something I'm missing. I'm still hoping I might have got this all wrong and there will be a simple explanation. Maybe Checkers will prove to be more of a Chatty Cathy than a cold-blooded killer and give me some much-needed answers.

I sip on my coffee, but the caffeine only makes me more jittery and my driving more hazardous. If I keep this up, I'll end up causing an accident. An Uber is beginning to look like the more pragmatic option. I've brought some cash with me in a money belt, hoping it will loosen Checkers' tongue, but I'm having second thoughts about that tactic. If I'm caught up in some kind of sting operation, I'm going to have a hard time talking my way out of it if I've just handed Checkers a fistful of cash.

Halfway into the drive, I'm starting to doubt that the GPS is taking me in the right direction. I was sure the address would be in a sleazy part of town, but it appears my destination is in an affluent neighborhood. Could Checkers be a suburban mom or dad selling drugs to their peers? It makes sense that Warren wouldn't want to buy drugs off some gang-infested street. At least I'm not risking my life driving out here.

The other possibility is that I'm completely wrong about Checkers' identity. I made the assumption that this individual is a dealer, but the name could mean virtually anything. Warren and I have been talking for the better part of a year now about getting a dog. Maybe Checkers is a breeder, and Warren was going to surprise me for my birthday next month. I quickly karate chop that idea out of existence. It doesn't jive with the part about my husband drugging me.

After draining my sixteen-ounce mug of coffee, I realize I need to find a bathroom before I arrive at my destination. I pull into the next gas station and hurry inside. My stomach is roiling with nerves and I'm half afraid I might throw up. I take a few minutes to compose myself and study my face in the mirror. A haggard-looking, middle-aged woman in need of a fix stares back at me. Frighteningly convincing for my undercover gig. I won't have to work hard to convince Checkers that I'm desperate to buy whatever they're selling.

After climbing back into the car, I check my route again. I'm only a few miles away from Acacia. This is definitely not the kind of neighborhood I anticipated. I'm starting to feel underdressed as I wheel past BMWs and Escalades parked in driveways. At least my Lexus won't be in any danger of being stripped of the stylish alloy wheels Warren bought me for Christmas.

Minutes later, I pull onto West Acacia Boulevard and roll to a stop a few doors down from 4517. I sit for a minute or two, deep breathing, and holding my fingers out in front of me to make sure they're not shaking too badly. I strap my gun to my waist and pat the wad of cash in my trouser pocket, wishing I'd brought a purse with me after all. I'm dressed too sloppily for this impromptu visit, and I didn't even bother applying make-up this morning.

I climb out and wend my way up the long driveway to the front door, admiring the manicured garden and trickling stone fountain. If Checkers is supplying drugs to the middle class, they appear to be doing a roaring trade. I ring the doorbell and chew on my lip as I listen to the elegant chime that follows.

The door opens, and my jaw drops at the face that greets me.

CHAPTER 56

"Luna!" I gasp. "What . . . what are you doing here?" I feel as though my mind is splintering. Is she the infamous Checkers? Was Luna supplying drugs to Warren? Or is there someone else in the house? I stare at her, registering the fact that her face is completely free of bruising, which seems virtually impossible considering the extent of her injuries.

Luna narrows her eyes at me, then throws a surreptitious glance over my shoulder as though expecting someone else. "Did you come alone?" she asks.

"Yes. I don't understand. Do you live here?"

She folds her arms in front of her. "I don't have to explain myself to you. You shouldn't have come here."

"I need answers. I'm looking for someone called Checkers."

She moves to close the door on me, but I quickly pull out my gun and point it at her. "I wouldn't do that if I were you."

Her face contorts in fear. She blinks rapidly, her grip on the door loosening. Before she can make another move, I shove past her and slam the door shut behind me. I turn around to face her, shocked at how calm I feel. Here I am pointing a gun at another human being, and not even flinching. I'm going through the motions like a well-oiled machine.

"It's time you and I had a conversation, Luna — if that's even your real name."

Without a word, she turns and leads me down the hallway into the kitchen. I pull the blinds shut and gesture for her to take a seat at the table. I sit down opposite her and lay the gun down in front of me in a slow, deliberate movement. "Now, why don't you start at the beginning and tell me exactly what's going on?"

Luna studies my expression, as though trying to gauge how much I already know, and how far I'm prepared to go, to get the information out of her. Silence ensues, as she continues to stare at me, her lips tightly sealed.

I let out a heavy sigh and run a finger over the barrel of my gun. Time to try my hand at a little bluffing. "I already know more than you think I do, Luna. There's a lot of evidence against you. The police suspect you of killing your stepfather, and you're about to be caught up in the investigation into Beth's disappearance too."

"I had nothing to do with that. I don't know where she is."

"Then you'd better start talking. You're in a whole lot of trouble, and I'm the only person who can help you. I'm the only one who was imprisoned in that house with you. I know what Gary did to you."

"I'm not going down for this. I didn't kill him. You did." She juts out her lip. "Exactly like you were supposed to."

I throw her an incredulous look. "Are you saying you set me up?"

She shrugs. "Somebody had to do it."

"I didn't kill him," I say. "I stabbed him in the side with the knife you left me, but someone else stabbed him in the chest after I fled. Your fingerprints are all over that place. The police may be acting like they're grateful for your cooperation, but they're looking at you as a person of interest."

"It wasn't me." She gives a careless shrug. "They can't prove anything."

I lean forward, fixing a stern expression on my face. "If it wasn't you, then who was it? If you don't come clean about everything, you're going to go down for murder. The coroner concluded that a different knife was used for the second stab wound. I'm off the hook, so that only leaves you."

"Or your husband," Luna counters.

I lean back in my chair, my breathing growing shallow. It's not as if I didn't suspect as much myself, but I was hoping Luna would confess to stabbing Gary, so I didn't have to face the horrifying reality that my husband's been lying to me. "Why did you text Warren your address? Are you trying to blackmail him?"

Her brows shoot up in surprise. "About what?"

"You just accused him of stabbing Gary. Maybe you were in the house and watched him do it. You saw a chance to make some money. I don't care about any of that. I just want the truth." I pause and gaze at her with a pleading look. "I want to know if my husband killed Gary."

She rests her elbows on the table, the hint of a smile playing on her lips. "I guess he must have, if you didn't."

"So, if you're not blackmailing Warren, why did you text him your address?"

She locks eyes with me, and I see it in the slight softening of her expression, the flush of her cheeks, the defiant tilt of her head — she's the other woman.

CHAPTER 57

I wait for a fireball of rage to rush through my veins, but instead my blood ices over. I remain still as a statue, waiting for my body to react to this devastating epiphany in some palpable manner. Time seems to freeze as I try to take it in. I can't believe I actually thought Checkers was a drug dealer. I should have realized it was way too saccharine a name to have any street cred. How on earth did Warren come up with such a ridiculous nickname for his illicit lover? Did they meet playing checkers in a coffee shop or something? A sour taste rises up the back of my throat. I don't even want to know the tawdry details. I'm just trying to absorb the shock of it all, without actually feeling anything — pretending as though my world hasn't just imploded. I can't get my head around the idea that Warren, my straightlaced, law-abiding husband, has been carrying on with a girl half his age. Is this really happening? Do I have it all wrong again? I take a deep breath, gratified when my voice holds steady, my tone neither accusatory nor defeated. "Are you sleeping with my husband?"

Luna gives a smug nod, evidently basking in my misery.

I try to ignore the sting of tears threatening to shed. "How long has it been going on?"

She tugs indifferently at her ponytail. "A little over a year."

Despite my best efforts, a horrified gasp slips out. I was expecting her to say a few weeks — a couple of months, tops. How could I have missed the signs all this time? How did I let this happen under my own nose? I squeeze my prickling eyes shut, determined not to cry in front of this girl who's made a mockery of my kindness. The hardest part is knowing that my husband was quite happy for the police to believe I killed Gary. Now I know why he was so eager to find the knife I used — he, or Luna, wanted to use it to finish Gary off so they could pin everything on me. *Exactly like you were supposed to.* That was the plan all along, and Luna was in on it.

"You and Warren were willing to let me go to prison for killing Gary," I say, as the dots begin to connect. "Except it didn't work out that way. Because I didn't kill him like you wanted me to. One of the two of you had to finish him off. You do realize you're going to go down for this, Luna? Warren's not going to take it on the chin for you. You're nothing but a piece on the side to him. So, if there's anything else you need to tell me, now would be the time."

Her eyes flash with anger. "It wasn't supposed to go down like this."

I casually curl a finger around the trigger of my gun. "Okay, how exactly was it supposed to go down?"

"You were supposed to die."

CHAPTER 58

"Tell me everything," I say, glaring across the table at Luna. "Start at the beginning."

She eyes the gun in front of me nervously. "Warren and I met at a seminar. I was working for a promotional company as a marketing rep. He was—"

"I know what he was working as," I interrupt. "Just get to the point."

She tosses her head indignantly. "As I was going to say, he was standing by himself at the beverage station the first time I saw him. He looked utterly miserable." One corner of her lip creeps upward in what I perceive to be a triumphant smirk.

"Go on," I say, in a tone dripping with disapproval.

"I engaged him in conversation, and I could tell at once he was interested in me. We clicked from the outset. He told me all about his soul-sucking marriage. Our affair started that very night."

My cheeks flush, but before I have a chance to interject, Luna goes on.

"Warren said he was tired of being married to a controlling, overbearing woman who stuck her nose into everyone

203

else's affairs." She tinkles a laugh. "I was a welcome reprieve in contrast."

Before I realize what's happening, I have the gun in my hands and I'm pointing it at Luna. Only this time my hands are shaking.

The cocky grin instantly slides from her face, and she scoots her chair backward, raising her palms in front of her. "Hey! Take it easy! You said to tell you everything. It's not my fault you don't like what you're hearing."

I lower the gun and set it back down on the table. I have no intention of shooting her, but it feels good to make her quiver in her boots. "Just stick to the facts, and I might not feel the urge to use you as target practice. Tell me about Warren's plan to kill me."

Luna cocks her head to one side. "Where to begin? At first, he talked about divorcing you, only it would have cost too much. He said you would fight him for years and try to take everything. In the end, he decided it would be worth the risk of getting rid of you to benefit from the hefty life insurance you insisted on purchasing when you got married." She tweaks another gloating grin. "We could use it when we start our family."

I ignore the merciless dig, even though it's tearing me up inside. I don't want to waste time exchanging insults. I'm more interested in drilling down on the details of Warren's nefarious plan. "How does Gary come into the picture? I take it he's not really your stepfather?"

Luna laughs. "Not even close. Warren didn't want to get his hands dirty, so he hired a fixer. He told him what he wanted to happen and left it up to him to figure out the finer points. The fixer came back with several options, and once he learned that you guys had a rental house next door, he suggested moving the hitman in to make it easier to take care of business. The plan was to stage a home invasion with you as the victim. Gary would get to stay on rent-free for one year afterward."

My heart surges up my throat. I knew the very first time I met Gary that there was something reprehensible about him. Like he knew things about me he shouldn't.

"And Beth?" I probe. "Was she part of the plot?"

Luna shrugs. "She was Gary's girlfriend."

"Do you know where she is, or what happened to her?" "No."

I throw a wary glance at the doorway. "Are you sure you're not lying to me? She's not living here, is she?"

Luna shakes her head. "No. This is an Airbnb. I rented it for a couple of weeks — Warren loaned me his credit card." She smiles blithely at me.

Of course he's funding it. A temporary love nest until he gets his hands on the life insurance, no doubt.

"So why didn't Gary kill me?" I ask.

"He was supposed to get rid of you weeks ago," Luna replies. "But he got greedy. He upped his fee and kept stalling on the job. Warren agreed to pay him an additional hundred grand. He gave him one more week to get the job done. Gary came up with a new plan to abduct you and bury you out in the desert somewhere. He said the home invasion was too risky because Maria Torres was becoming suspicious of him. Warren asked me to help lure you into the rental. It was my idea to put the sign in the window." She grins at me again, as though expecting me to be impressed by her ingenuity.

I reach for the gun again and the congratulatory smile on her lips evaporates. "Keep going," I say.

"Once Gary had you tied up, he tried to negotiate for even more money. Warren knew he had to get rid of him — he'd become more trouble than he was worth. That's when he came up with the plan for me to sneak you a knife. We figured one or the other of you would end up dead, and the other would go down for it."

I'm seething inwardly, but I force myself to remain calm until I can gather all the information I need. "I take it your bruises were fake?"

She chuckles, looking pleased with herself again. "I found a great YouTube tutorial on injury and wound make-up."

I fall silent for a few minutes as I weigh my options. I don't believe Luna's story in its entirety. It's her word against Warren's when it comes to who killed Gary. Someone's going to prison for it, but it isn't going to be me. I need to play this strategically. "If you agree to tell the police that you saw Warren stab Gary, I'll back you up as another one of Gary's victims. Personally, I'd prefer to see my husband serve a life sentence, but it wouldn't hurt my feelings if you took his place. Your choice."

Her eyes drift to the gun once more. "Okay, I'll do it."

I give a curt nod. "First, I'm going to need the fixer's number. If your story doesn't check out, the terms of our agreement will change."

CHAPTER 59

I feign total shock when the cops arrive at the house to arrest Warren. He's not the only one of us who can perform on cue. I watch from behind the drapes at the family room window as my handcuffed husband is escorted to the curb. One of the officers places a protective hand over Warren's head as he climbs into the back seat of the squad car, still protesting his innocence. My guess is that they'll charge him with second-degree murder, and possibly attempted murder. Luna's testimony about the plot to kill me proved to be compelling. Even though the fixer has disappeared into thin air, I'm hoping the police will be able to restore the deleted messages between him and Warren. At this stage, I'm not sure I even care if it was Warren or Luna who stabbed Gary to death. The fact that one of them will pay the price is enough to satisfy my appetite for retribution.

After the squad cars leave, I sling my purse over my shoulder and walk down the street to Amber's house. Now that it's finally over, I need to debrief with someone I trust.

"You look terrible," she says, eyeing me up and down when she opens the door.

"I'm not exactly on cloud nine," I reply morosely.

"Can I make you some coffee, or do you need something stronger?" she asks, leading me to the kitchen.

I pull out a stool at the island. "I need caffeine. Make it a strong one."

"I saw the cop cars going down the street," she says, fussing with the coffee maker. "Were they searching your house again?"

"Worse. They arrested Warren."

She spins around to face me, her features slack with shock. "For what?"

"Murder."

Amber sets a steaming mug of coffee in front of me and slumps down next to me. "I don't understand. I thought Luna killed Gary."

I hang my purse on the back of the bar stool and take a welcome sip of coffee. "She denies it. She says she saw Warren lunge at Gary with a knife right before she fled the house."

"How did she escape? I thought you said Gary kept her tied up in one of the bathrooms."

"I'm not sure. I don't know if Warren freed her, or if she managed to get ahold of another knife and freed herself."

Amber shakes her head in a disbelieving fashion. "I can't picture Warren killing someone. He's so . . . docile. Luna, on the other hand — she hated her stepfather. And if she thought for one minute that he'd killed her mom—"

"Beth wasn't her mom," I interrupt. "And Gary wasn't her stepfather."

Amber's tapered brows shoot upward. "What are you talking about?"

"There's a lot you don't know. And a lot I didn't know about my own husband either." I scrunch my eyes shut briefly before continuing. "It turns out Warren's been having an affair with Luna. She told me he'd decided it was too expensive to divorce me and he was plotting to kill me instead. He went through a middleman — a fixer — to hire Gary Finkel to get rid of me."

208

Amber gasps. "What? I don't believe it. Luna's lying to you. Warren's not that devious."

"Devious enough to have a year-long affair behind my back. And he's been drugging me. That's why I was having all those hallucinations." I wrap my fingers around my coffee cup and blow on the surface gently. "The police have confiscated Warren's phone and computer. They're bound to find evidence of the plot to kill me. Even if they can't prove he killed Gary, they can get him for conspiracy to murder with Luna's testimony."

Amber frowns. "I just can't believe this is happening. It's like one of those crazy crime show specials you see on TV. What are you going to do if Warren makes bail?"

I sip my coffee, contemplating my answer. My thoughts go to the gun I locked back up in the safe. I know what I'd like to do, but I have no intention of going to prison. "I'm filing for divorce," I tell her. "That's as far as I've got."

* * *

Warren is released on bail the following day. He actually has the gall to call me from the station and ask me to pick him up.

"Get an Uber to a hotel," I snap, before ending the call.

I'm pacing across the kitchen floor when he shows up at the back door an hour later. He stares at me with an irritated look on his face, waiting on me to unlock it. He's not supposed to be here, according to the terms of his bail, but the truth is I desperately want to know why he did what he did, and I want to hear it directly from him. I had no idea he was unhappy in our relationship. Some foolish part of my heart wants to believe that everything Luna told me was a lie. But I won't be duped a second time. I take a moment to retrieve the gun from the safe, then return to the door to let Warren in. Weapon in hand, I lead him through to the kitchen, then sit back down at the table without saying a word. I want to see how much truth he volunteers before I tell him what I know.

"I didn't do it," he begins, taking a seat opposite me.

I eye him coldly. He's not going to make it easy for me. "Do *what*, Warren?"

He scratches the stubble on his jaw. "I didn't kill Gary. He was already dead when I went over there. Luna must have stabbed him."

"Don't lie to me. I know all about your affair with her."

His mouth drops open, as though he's about to protest, but then he stretches his hands toward me in a pleading fashion. "Kay, that was the biggest mistake of my life. But I didn't kill Gary. It was her. You have to believe me. She has it in for me because I tried to break things off with her."

I curl my lip at him in disgust. "Don't bother with your lies, Warren. I spoke with Luna. I know everything. You've been drugging me so that everyone would think I was losing the plot when I aired my suspicions about Gary. I even found your online pharmacy order. Did you really think you would get away with this? You lured me next door to have me murdered. You have some nerve installing a hitman in the rental house we bought with my parents' money!"

"Don't be ridiculous, Kay! You're hallucinating again."

I jump to my feet and point the gun at his chest. "I want you out. Now. I'll leave your stuff at the curb with the trash, where you belong."

"Fine! If that's how you want it." Warren gets to his feet slowly, sneering at me. "Lucky break for you that your mom left that burner on, or you'd never have gotten the money for the rental in the first place."

He walks over to the door, then turns and gives me a malicious wink before exiting the house.

CHAPTER 60

I sit at the kitchen island, pulsing with rage, long after Warren has slammed the door behind him. Reels of memories play back in my mind as I try to decide if my husband just confessed to murdering my parents, or if he was simply taunting me. All this time I was worried I might have rented the house next door to a serial killer, but what if I've been married to one all along? It was shocking to learn from the fire investigator that Mom had accidentally left a burner on. She didn't have dementia, but it wasn't beyond the realm of possibility — most of us have forgotten to turn a stove off at one time or another. Even the police didn't question it. After all, my mother was eighty years old. But she was a stickler for safety. It was out of character for her to forget something so critical.

My hands shake as I open the refrigerator and reach for a bottle of pinot grigio. I don't like drinking alone, but tonight I need something to settle my fraying nerves. In my mind, I'm combing back through the past year, questioning everything Warren has said and done. How long has he been gaslighting me? Looking back, I realize he was the one who encouraged me to run for HOA president in the first place. Not that he ever came to any of the meetings. I suspect it was just another opportunity for him to carry on with Luna behind my back. All that praise he kept heaping on me about being so good at the job and putting in all those hours served him well. I can't help wondering if Luna ever came to our house while I was at the clubhouse conducting HOA meetings or organizing committees. Surely Warren wouldn't have taken the risk of being discovered. He must have met her in a hotel, or maybe she lived nearby — no doubt in an apartment we were paying for, unbeknownst to me.

I fill my wine glass to the top, then set the bottle down on the table next to me, almost jumping out of my skin when the doorbell rings. My first thought is that Warren has come back with a weapon, demanding I let him in. Fear ripples through my veins. I don't think he took his key with him, but I could be mistaken. I dart into the family room and peer furtively through the window at a cop car parked at the curb. Another unwelcome visitor. Grimacing, I dash to the safe and lock the gun away again before making my way to the front door.

"Officer Engelmann, how can I help you?"

He gives a tight smile. "Can I come in for a minute?"

I shrug indifferently, and usher him into the kitchen.

His eyes flick to the open bottle of wine, but he doesn't comment on it.

"I'd offer you a glass," I say, "but I assume you're on duty."

He clears his throat, pinning a penetrating gaze on me. "Do you know where Luna Webster is?"

"I already gave the police the address of the Airbnb she's staying at."

He rubs his jaw. "She's not there anymore. She checked out early this morning, according to the homeowner."

Blood drains from my head. This can't be happening. I need Luna to testify against Warren. We had a deal. Without her testimony, I'm under as big a cloud of suspicion as Warren is. There's only one reason why she's disappeared. She killed Gary, and she knows it's only a matter of time before the police find her DNA on the murder weapon.

"I have no idea where she is." I rub my hands over my face and groan in frustration. "What happens now? She was the only witness we had."

Engelmann studies me with a shrewd look, presumably wondering whether he can believe me or not. After all, I didn't come clean about everything from the beginning. He had to dig the information about the knife out of me. For all he knows, I could be hiding a whole lot more.

I could be protecting the murderer of the hitman hired to kill me.

CHAPTER 61

At midnight, I'm still wide awake even after polishing off an entire bottle of wine, so I throw myself down on the couch in front of the TV and reach for the remote. I can't lie in bed staring at the ceiling all night, tormenting myself with thoughts of Warren's betrayal. I'd rather fall asleep watching some mind-numbingly boring TV show — my second drug of choice. I turn the volume down and find a low-budget B-movie that I've never heard of, but which is pretty much guaranteed to put me to sleep, if the description is anything to go by. My eyelids soon drift to half-mast and the remote begins to slip from my fingers. I turn the TV off and curl up in a ball on my side.

Several hours later, I wake with a start, sensing something, or someone, moving around in the house. It's dark in the room, apart from the ghoulish green glow of the equipment rack below the TV. I blink, listening for any sounds, creaks in the floor, but silence prevails. Was I dreaming? My heart begins a skittish beat. What if Warren came back in the middle of the night to finish me off? Surely, he wouldn't dare break into the house — not when he's out on bail facing charges of murder and conspiracy to murder.

I breathe slowly in and out, quietly adjusting my position. My neck is aching after being wedged against a particularly uncomfortable cushion that looked good in the store. Slowly, I sit up and squint around the room, allowing my eyes to grow accustomed to the shadowy darkness. There's no one here. It's just my imagination. I punch the cushion under me and lay back down, but I can't relax. Even though I can't hear or see anyone, I can sense a presence in the house with me. I wet my parched lips and sit up again. This time, I switch on the lamp on the end table and scan the room to make sure I'm alone. I remind myself that all the doors are locked. I'm safe in my own home. Gary is dead, and Warren is holed up in some fleabag hotel, snoring his head off.

Luna!

My heart surges up my throat. Did she come back to kill me too? She double-crossed me — bailed on me after promising to testify against Warren. She must hold it against me that I forced her hand, guaranteeing prison time for her lover and the death of their relationship as she knew it. If she killed Gary, she'll have no qualms about killing me too. I scramble to my feet, adrenaline thundering through my system like a wooden roller coaster. I need to get to the safe and retrieve my gun. This time, I won't hesitate to use it. I'm tired of being everyone else's target.

Gingerly, I pad across the floor to the hallway, racking my brain as I try to remember where I stashed the emergency flashlight. I need to call 911, but my phone is charging in the kitchen. The gun is in the safe in Warren's office, and it's closer. I creep stealthily down the dark hallway, trailing a hand along the wall to orient myself as I go. I can't shake the feeling that Luna is somewhere in the house, even though I keep telling myself it's absurd — there's no way she would risk coming back to finish what she and Warren started.

I make it safely to the office and slip inside, closing the door softly behind me. For several agonizing minutes, I fumble with the lock before the door to the safe finally clicks open.

Before I can reach inside for the gun, a voice behind me says, "Hello, Kay."

CHAPTER 62

My legs give way beneath me, and I reach for the desk to steady myself. I peer into the shadowy darkness, bedlam swarming my brain. Am I seeing things — looking at a ghost? It can't be, can it? This must be another one of those wretched hallucinations. Did Warren manage to drug me tonight before he left for the hotel?

"I didn't expect you to be awake," Beth says, her voice surprisingly strong and unfaltering. She walks over to me and reaches for the gun. "You won't be needing this."

Frozen with fear, I watch as she closes the safe door and turns to face me.

"B . . . Beth. I . . . I thought you were dead."

She flaps a hand at me, her lip curling contemptuously. "Yeah, well. It had to look that way."

I'm vaguely aware that my mouth is hanging open, but I'm not sure how to frame the questions clamoring to be answered. I wait for Beth to explain herself, but instead she twists a lock of hair around her finger and plonks down on Warren's swivel chair. "I noticed you've been imbibing tonight. I could use a drink myself. What do you say we retire to the kitchen for our conversation?"

When I don't respond, she gets to her feet and walks toward the door. "A little hospitality's not too much to ask under the circumstances, is it?"

I'm not sure what circumstances she's referring to, or how much she knows about what went down in her absence. Does she know that Gary's dead? Stunned into silence, I follow her to the kitchen and reach for another bottle of pinot grigio.

"I prefer vodka," she says, arching a brow mockingly at me. "Have you forgotten?"

"I don't have any."

She shrugs and takes a seat at the kitchen island. "Fine, I'll have a red wine instead."

"I don't understand," I say, pouring her a glass of caber-net. "Why did you disappear without telling me? You knew I would have helped you — all you had to do was ask. Did Gary try to kill you too? Larry's his real name, right?"

She throws back her head and laughs. "He goes by Gary now. We almost killed each other a couple of times. I have to admit, it was hard not to get irritated when he finished my sentences for me, but pretending to be vegetarian is what almost did me in." She reaches for her glass and cocks her head to one side. "Apart from that, this was a pretty easy job. At least, until you killed Gary."

She locks her gaze on me, drilling into my soul with a darkness I've never seen in anyone's eyes before. Instinctively, I take a step backward. "You've got it all wrong, Beth. I didn't kill him. It was Luna. Warren was in on it too. They've been lying to me about everything. They were having an affair."

"Don't whine to me. I couldn't care less about the state of your crummy marriage. That's not why I came back." Beth narrows her eyes. "I know you stabbed Gary. You admitted it to the police." Her accusing tone is like a hand plunging into my chest and ripping my heart out. All I ever wanted to do was help her. Everything that happened was because I cared enough to ask questions about a woman I thought was being abused.

"I had no choice, Beth. He was going to kill me. That's what Warren hired him to do. They lured me over there by pretending Gary was holding Luna prisoner. When Gary demanded more money, Warren and Luna decided it would be easier to get rid of him. They set me up. Luna sneaked a knife into my room. They were counting on me attacking him in a bid to escape. I caught him by surprise, but it was only a superficial wound. Luna stabbed him in the chest after I fled. Warren and Luna wanted me to go down for his murder. You have to believe me, Beth."

She furrows her brow, a contemplative look on her face. "The problem is, we never got our money."

The cogs in my brain whir as the words slowly sink in. "*Our* money? You knew?"

"Of course I knew," she replies, with an impatient toss of her head. "I thought I made it clear to you that the abused wife part was all an act. We had to paint you as the unhinged neighbor who was constantly interfering in our marriage and accusing Gary of secretly murdering me and disposing of my body, even though I'm very much alive, as you can see." She studies her painted nails for a moment. "All I have to do is show myself to the police to prove you're a lunatic who attacked my husband for no reason."

My insides are jiggling like jelly, but I jut my chin out in defiance. "If you do that, you'll never get justice for Gary's death. And you'll never see a penny of your money."

As I'd hoped, the mention of money grabs her attention. Her eyes glitter as she reaches for her glass. She takes a long draft, her gaze never leaving mine. "What exactly are you suggesting?"

I open another bottle of pinot grigio and tell her my plan.

CHAPTER 63

As it turns out, Beth was very receptive to my proposition. She likes the idea of living next door rent-free and having me at her beck and call. She even dropped off a bottle of vodka so we can celebrate after we've executed our plan. I've spent the past forty-eight hours perfecting it and combing through it again to make sure I've thought of everything. Warren is coming over this evening to ostensibly pick up his personal items and hammer out some of the financial details of our divorce. A pointless exercise — but he doesn't need to know that. I've gone out of my way to make the house look as messy as possible just to trigger him. And I've put all his stuff in garbage bags and dumped them at the curb by way of greeting. A petty gesture, but infinitely satisfying.

When the doorbell rings, I arrange my expression into one of placid neutrality. Despite what he's done, I need Warren to think this meeting is going to go in his favor.

"Evening," he says, with a tightly wound smile, when I open the door.

I don't bother returning his hollow greeting. "Just so you know, I'm recording your visit for my own safety. Cameras are tracking your every move."

He follows me into the family room and scowls when I motion for him to take a seat. I hold up my phone and tap my fingernail on the screen. "I'm ready to dial 911 in a nano-second, so don't even think about trying any funny business."

He turns his back on me and begins leafing through the pile of bank statements tossed haphazardly across the glass coffee table. "It's starting to rain," he says. "I should load my stuff before we start on this, or it'll get soaked."

"It can wait. I want to get the paperwork out of the way, and you out of my house, as quickly as possible," I reply brusquely.

Warren's eyes skate disapprovingly around the disarray in the room. "The place looks like a pigsty already."

"I prefer a more organic look," I say, suppressing a grin as I reach for a sheaf of financial statements.

"My lawyer hasn't had a chance to look those over," Warren whines. "I'm going to need every penny I have to defend myself."

"Lawyers will just drag things out so they can pad their own pockets," I say. "How about we keep things simple and agree to a fifty-fifty split on the savings, checking, and credit card balances?"

Warren frowns. "I need to go back through the credit card statements first and see what was purchased. I don't see why I should be responsible for half of your personal charges."

"Have at it." I sink back in my chair, watching as he pores over the statements, muttering to himself. I used to admire how meticulous Warren was about everything. Now I'm see-ing him in a different light — as the narcissist he really is, completely disinterested in anyone's welfare but his own.

Deep in thought, I almost jump out of my skin when the door bursts open and Beth steps into the room, pointing a gun at us. Even though I choreographed the entire scene down to the smallest detail, my eyes involuntarily widen in shock. Beth's gaze is as chilling as blackened steel. The wom-an's ability to morph into character is truly frightening. I can't help wondering if I might have made a pact with the grim reaper herself. I only hope she comes through with her end of the bargain and doesn't kill me afterward to keep me from talking. The disturbing thought burrows like a drill deep into my brain.

Warren attempts to get to his feet, but Beth gestures with the gun for him to stay put. "Don't even think about it." She shuts the door behind her, then closes the blinds. "It's time I had a chat with my neighbors about how we're going to handle things moving forward."

She walks over to the mantel and leans against it, facing us with a peculiar grin on her face.

"What are you doing here?" Warren seethes, his face blotchy with rage. "You weren't supposed to come back."

Her nostrils twitch like a horse getting ready to charge. "And Gary wasn't supposed to die either."

"Please, Beth," I squeak, holding up my hands in a suitably pitiful manner. "We'll give you whatever you want. Just put down the gun."

"We had a deal," Warren blusters. "Gary reneged on it. What did you think was going to happen?"

Beth's eyes glitter with wrath, or greed, or some combination of the seven sins. "I thought I was going to get paid, for starters."

"Well, you blew that one," Warren scoffs. "You and your money-grabbing cohort in crime. Thanks to you, I'm going to need all the cash I can get my hands on to fight these charges."

Beth taps a finger to her temple thoughtfully. "Maybe we can rethink that. I have a proposal for you."

CHAPTER 64

Warren eyes Beth warily from beneath narrowed brows. "What do you have in mind?"

"A mutually beneficial trade that gives us both what we want. I'll agree to swear it was Luna who stabbed Gary, and in return, you pay me every last penny you owe us."

Warren squeezes his jaw, his face knotted in contemplation. "We agreed to fifty thousand, plus one year of rent-free living in the house."

"I'm not talking about the initial agreement. I want the amount you killed him over," Beth says. "Double or nothing."

I tug on Warren's sleeve. "You can't agree to this. It's blackmail. If the police find out you lied to frame Luna, you're going to end up in even more trouble than you're already in."

"It's not your freedom that's at stake," he growls, shrugging me off him, before turning his attention back to Beth. "I don't have that kind of liquid cash."

"Perhaps we can come up with some kind of payment plan. After all, now that you won't be going to prison, you'll be able to keep your job." She throws a derisive look in my direction. "That's if you can get your wife on board. What do you say, Kay? It's either that or face the stigma for the rest of your life of being married to a convicted murderer."

222

Warren turns to me. "You heard her. What's it going to be? Either you agree to Beth's terms, or I'll take you down with me."

"That's not going to happen," I say. "Not when the jury hears how you planned to have me killed."

"No jury's going to believe your wild tale about your husband scheming with a hitman to take you out when I show up in court as a witness for the defense," Beth says, with a knowing smirk.

She stares me down and I dutifully drop my gaze. Except I'm not pretending to be intimidated — I am intimidated. Once again, I question whether I've done the right thing by joining forces with Beth. I'm not well-versed in the workings of the criminal mind, but I'm fairly certain she would double-cross me in a nanosecond if it resulted in more money or bigger benefits to her.

I cover my face with my hands and pretend to be anguished over the decision I'm being forced to make. "Okay, I'll do it," I say, with a heavy sigh. "Under the condition that Warren signs both of the houses over to me."

Beth shrugs. "You two can fight all you want about the nitty-gritty. So, do we have a deal?"

Warren gives a curt nod. "We do."

"In that case," Beth continues, "let's make it official." She pulls out a folded piece of paper and flattens it on the coffee table in front of Warren, then places her phone next to it. "I'll need you to read and record this confession as surety, so you don't try to turn me in for blackmail later."

Warren thumps a fist on the table. "Are you out of you mind? I'm not recording anything of the sort for you."

Beth flicks an imaginary piece of fluff from her sleeve, seemingly unperturbed. "Your choice. But don't waste my time. If you're not interested in dealing on my terms, then I'll throw my weight behind Luna's side of the story."

"Don't do it," I whisper to Warren, my eyes wide and pleading.

He glares at me and reaches for Beth's phone. "Stay out of this. You have no idea what you're talking about."

I turn my head to one side to hide my smile as he begins recording his confession. When he's finished, he hands Beth her phone. "You got what you wanted. Guess we're partners now."

"I'm glad we could come to a satisfactory agreement," she replies. "What do you say we toast our new alliance?" She glances over at me. "Got any vodka?"

"In the kitchen," I say, getting to my feet. I return a couple of minutes later with the bottle and three glasses. Beth pours us each a generous shot. My hand is shaking as we clink glasses.

Beth raises hers in a toast. "To Luna taking the fall for one and all."

"May the best con artist win," Warren adds, downing his drink.

"That would be me, and I already did," I say, setting down my untouched glass and waiting for the inevitable.

CHAPTER 65

Warren slumps sideways first. I reach into my pocket and pull out an empty pill box. He watches me with the fixed stare of the terminally ill, his limbs motionless apart from an occasional, reflexive twitch. I feel no sympathy for him. He gets to die a painless death. I only hope my parents didn't suffer.

"I know you have questions, Warren, and I know you're unable to articulate them right now, so let me go ahead and answer them for you. You overdosed. You couldn't live with what you'd done." I smile congenially at him. "Fortunately for me, you recorded a confession first — the final, selfless act of a suicidal man clearing his conscience."

There's a loud thump behind us as Beth crumples to the floor.

Warren's unfocused gaze skates around the room as though trying to locate her before his eyes roll back in his head.

My gun has slipped from Beth's grasp. I see her strain to try and reach it, but her fingers betray her, immobile and defeated against a deadly combination of hallucinogens, sleeping pills and muscle relaxants. I walk over to her and crouch down next to her. She stares fixedly up at me, then gives an almost imperceptible nod. I like to think she's trying to convey how impressed she is at how skillfully I played her. I'm not stupid enough to leave any witnesses, especially not one as cunning as she has proven to be. I watch as she slowly fades from consciousness. Bye-bye, Beth, I mouth. You're not going to be a financial burden going forward. More important, you're not going to be my next-door neighbor ever again.

I've already figured out how I'm going to dispose of her body. She disappeared over a month ago, purportedly while in rehab, so no one's going to be looking for her. I'll wrap her in a duvet, dump her in a wheelbarrow, and bury her at the bottom of the rental house garden. If she's ever found, it will only confirm what everyone suspected — that Gary got rid of her. Sometimes, it pays to spread rumors.

I walk over to my husband and check his pulse. He's still breathing, but barely. I consider holding a cushion to his face to speed up the process, but the autopsy would betray me. I need to be patient and sit with him until he exhales his last. When he does, I'll take my one remaining sleeping pill and go to bed. In the morning, I'll pretend to discover his body and call for an ambulance in a suitably distraught manner.

Sinking into a chair, I pull a woolen blanket around my shoulders. The wind is howling outside now, and the swing on the porch creaks eerily every few minutes or so. A fitting setting for my ghoulish deeds. I'm sure Warren's stuff is drenched by now — not that he'll be needing dry clothes any time soon.

As my husband's breathing grows raspier, I scroll idly through my phone to distract myself, pausing briefly at Amber's name. I'm tempted to call her, but I can't burden my best friend with the awful things I've done tonight. I'm not sure how it has come down to this. For once, I wish I were hallucinating. All this time, I suspected I was living next door to a serial killer, only to find out that I was married to one. And now, I am one. It's not a role I set out to play. There must be something in the air on this street. I really need to get away from here and make a fresh start. Maybe I should leave an anonymous tip on the police hotline, leading them to Beth's body. No one would blame me for wanting to get away from here after such a horrific discovery in my renter's garden, and no one would ever suspect the HOA president of murder.

I continue browsing through my contacts, wishing there was someone I could call, someone who would understand me, and not judge me — someone who wouldn't be burdened by so heavy a confession. Keeping secrets makes for a lonely life, which explains why most are spilled over time.

I stop scrolling when I come to the fixer's number. I'd forgotten I put that in my phone. I should probably get rid of it, now that I won't be needing it anymore. I hesitate, my finger hovering above the delete button. Maybe I should keep it a little longer. After all, Luna's still out there somewhere, and she doesn't know, yet, that Warren is dead. Who knows how she'll take the news? She's already plunged a knife into one man's chest. I'll wager it only whet her appetite for more. I close the contacts app on my phone and get to my feet, stifling a yawn.

Best to hold on to the fixer's number for another rainy day.

THE END

THE END

AUTHOR'S NOTE

Dear Reader,

I hope you enjoyed reading this book as much as I enjoyed writing it.

One question I am often asked is where I get my ideas from. The answer is a fertile imagination! I was always the kid who got elected to tell the scary bedtime stories at sleepovers. Whenever I babysat as a teenager I would make up stories for the kids and leave them on a cliffhanger to make sure I was invited back. I'm grateful that the ideas keep coming to this day.

Thank you so much for taking the time to check out my books, and I would appreciate it from the bottom of my heart if you would leave a review on Amazon or Goodreads as it makes a HUGE difference in helping new readers find the series. If you enjoy fast-paced, well-crafted, psychological suspense mysteries — clean enough to recommend to your mother-in-law, but compelling enough to keep you reading until two in the morning — I invite you to check out my website and join my newsletter to be the first to hear about my upcoming book releases, sales, and fun giveaways. You can also follow me on Twitter, Instagram, and Facebook. Feel free to email me at norma@normahinkens.com with any feedback or comments. I LOVE hearing from readers. YOU are the reason I keep writing!

All my best,
Norma

THE JOFFE BOOKS STORY

We began in 2014 when Jasper agreed to publish his mum's much-rejected romance novel and it became a bestseller.

Since then we've grown into the largest independent publisher in the UK. We're extremely proud to publish some of the very best writers in the world, including Joy Ellis, Faith Martin, Caro Ramsay, Helen Forrester, Simon Brett and Robert Goddard. Everyone at Joffe Books loves reading and we never forget that it all begins with the magic of an author telling a story.

We are proud to publish talented first-time authors, as well as established writers whose books we love introducing to a new generation of readers.

We won Trade Publisher of the Year at the Independent Publishing Awards in 2023 and Best Publisher Award in 2024 at the People's Book Prize. We have been shortlisted for Independent Publisher of the Year at the British Book Awards for the last five years, and were shortlisted for the Diversity and Inclusivity Award at the 2022 Independent Publishing Awards. In 2023 we were shortlisted for Publisher of the Year at the RNA Industry Awards, and in 2024 we were shortlisted at the CWA Daggers for the Best Crime and Mystery Publisher.

We built this company with your help, and we love to hear from you, so please email us about absolutely anything bookish at feedback@joffebooks.com.

If you want to receive free books every Friday and hear about all our new releases, join our mailing list here: www.joffebooks.com/freebooks.

And when you tell your friends about us, just remember: it's pronounced Joffe as in coffee or toffee!

www.ingramcontent.com/pod-product-compliance
Lightning Source LLC
Chambersburg PA
CBHW011518170626
46810CB00010B/3410